THE WHITE PICKET FENCE

KAREN ROSE

eISBN: 979-8-9917875-0-5

paperback ISBN: 979-8-9917875-1-2

audio ISBN: 979-8-9917875-2-9

Cover design by: Renee Fecher

To Robin Rue. Thank you for sticking by my side for the past nineteen years. Thank you for your wise counsel, for your unflagging enthusiasm, and for always having an encouraging word. But most of all, I thank you for your friendship.

And, as always, to Martin. I love you so very much.

LETTER TO READERS

Hello! I hope you all enjoy Tino Ciccotelli's story! Tino was first introduced in DIE FOR ME (2007). He also appears in DID YOU MISS ME (2013) and SAY YOU'RE SORRY (2019).

I felt it was high time for Tino to get his own happily ever after.

Tino's story is set nine years after DIE FOR ME and fifteen months after the free short "O HOLY NIGHT." You can find it on my website, karenrosebooks.com, under "For Readers."

I've wanted to revisit my old friends from the early books for some time now. Tino is just the first of many. Stay tuned for future novellas featuring the early characters!

And thank you all. If you're new to my books, I hope you love them. And if you've been around since the beginning or anywhere in between, I'm so very grateful for your support!

Best wishes always,
Karen Rose

CHAPTER 1

"Hey, Tino."

Tino Ciccotelli smiled at the nurse on duty at the ICU desk. "Mrs. G. So good to see you." And it was. Although Tino wished he'd seen her nearly anywhere else but here.

Here, in a hospital.

Tino had come to hate hospitals. Not that anyone liked them, of course.

Marian Gargano smiled back in that motherly way she had. She was his oldest friend's mom, and he'd spent more time at her kitchen table during his teen years than he had his own.

There had been a number of times over the years that he'd wished she were his mother.

The thought used to make him feel guilty, feel like he'd betrayed his own mother, but at the moment he was too tired to care.

She tilted her head, studying him. "You look exhausted."

"Because I am. Just got off a plane."

"Where were you off to this time?"

"Knoxville, Tennessee. Murder victim. I interviewed a child who witnessed her mom getting killed."

Her expression softened. "I'm so sorry, honey. I know those cases take it out of you."

They did. He met victims and their families at the worst times of their lives. It had begun to wear on him, the constant sorrow. Interviewing children—be they witnesses or victims—made the sorrow so much worse.

"Someone's got to do it." And that someone was him. He did what he did for the victims, for their families. He played a small part in getting them justice. "I was able to get a good sketch. Cops have already ID'd the killer."

Usually, he tried to take a break between interviews, but the request had come in the night before to get back to Philly for another victim. The woman he was here at the ICU to see was, thankfully, still alive to tell her own story.

D. Johnson, white female, age seventy-five. She'd been beaten within an inch of her life but had somehow survived. *Must be a tough old bird.*

Hopefully, her memories of her attacker would be crisp enough to be useful. Hopefully, Tino would be able to take those memories and turn them into a "wanted" poster.

Marian came around the desk to cup his cheek. "This one's going to be harder."

Tino frowned. Miss Johnson was the survivor of an assault. Not a sexual assault, thank the good Lord, because those were devastating. "Why?"

It was Marian's turn to frown. "It's Mrs. Johnson."

So a Mrs., not a Miss. "And?"

Marian's expression became confused. "Did you not read the file they sent?"

"I only got a name. D. Johnson."

"Dorothy Johnson, Tino. Your old art teacher from high school."

Tino felt his knees wobble and had to take a step back. "What?" he whispered, because Dorothy Johnson had been the first person to nurture his ability, to tell him that he was good, that he was really good.

She'd given him the confidence to pursue art as a career.

She was the reason he stood right here, right now.

"*She's* the victim?"

Marian nodded sadly. "She was attacked in her own home. Luckily Charlie has been checking on her nearly every day. She found her only about a half hour later."

Oh God. Charlie. No, not Charlie. Charlotte.

Once again Tino's knees wobbled. "Charlotte is here?"

She'd been his first kiss. His first love. His first heartbreak.

Marian's brows lifted slightly. "Oh. If I'd known you were in the dark, I'd have texted you. Given you the heads-up. When was the last time you saw Charlie?"

"Graduation. She went off to college and we parted ways." He shrugged. "Grew apart."

"Well, she's in there with Dorothy, so pull up your big boy pants and get your butt in there."

The command in Marian's tone almost made Tino smile. He'd heard that tone so many times as a teenager, usually because he and Cliff had gotten into some trouble or other.

And several of those times, Charlotte had been right in there with them. She'd been a good girl, but she'd liked adventure. Wanted out of Philly. Wanted to see the world. Wanted to be somebody.

Tino wondered if she'd gotten her wish.

"Yes, ma'am. But first, I have something for you." From his sketchbook, he pulled a single sheet, its edges finished and smooth. "Happy birthday, Mrs. G."

Marian took the portrait done in charcoal, her eyes suddenly glassy with tears. "Tino," she breathed. "It's . . . I have no words, son."

And he had no words every time she called him son. "Turned out okay, I guess."

She gazed at the portrait of her granddaughter, blinking once to send the tears in her eyes streaking down her cheeks. "You are magic."

He shrugged, uncomfortable with her praise. He was an artist. A pretty damn good one, if he said so himself. But to hear the woman who'd been more of a mother to him than his own had been say he was magic . . .

That was everything.

"Cliff made a pretty baby," he said.

She sniffled, wiping at her tears with the back of her hand. "I think Sonya had something to do with it."

Sonya and Cliff had become first-time parents ten months ago and Tino was little Addison's godfather. It was the first time he'd been a godfather to someone outside the Ciccotelli clan. Although Cliff was as much his brother as Dino, Gino, and Vito. Sonya was as much his sister as his own sister, Tess.

Cliff and Sonya and Tino and Charlotte. They'd all been joined at the hip in high school. Tino had assumed they'd all be together forever. Then Charlotte had gone away.

"Probably more than something," Tino allowed, "considering Addison's a carbon copy of Sonya as a baby." He sighed. "I need to go. I've stalled long enough."

He had to go in and see Mrs. Johnson. Hurt and scared. He didn't want to see her that way. He selfishly wanted to remember her as his high school art teacher with her colorful headscarves and flowing dresses and the bangles that sounded like little bells whenever she moved.

"Not stalling," Marian said kindly. "We all need to recharge every now and then, Tino." She cupped his cheek again. "You come see me at home, and I'll make you a pie."

"Cherry?" he asked hopefully.

"Would I make you anything else?"

He grinned at her and squared his shoulders. "Gotta work."

She hesitated. "She looks bad, Tino. Be prepared."

Tino swallowed and forced himself to ask the question he'd been dreading. "How bad?"

"She's here, kiddo, in the ICU. Her chances of survival are fifty-fifty."

Tino sucked in a breath. "She might die?"

Marian's smile was sad. "We hope not. We're giving her the best care possible."

"I know. Okay, then. Time to work."

"Room one fifteen. She asked us to reduce her pain meds so that she could be sharp for the police artist."

So she knew he was coming. Or at least that *a* police artist was coming. He hoped she'd be happy to see him. Or that he could at least give her some comfort. "Thanks, Mrs. G."

Bracing himself, Tino walked to Mrs. Johnson's room. He paused at the large window to get a read on the situation, which was his custom before interviewing an ICU victim. The rooms were mostly windows so that the nurses could keep eyes on their patients, so his view of Mrs. Johnson was unobstructed.

He sucked in a breath and let it out carefully. *Oh, Mrs. Johnson. I'm so sorry.*

Sorrow grabbed at his heart as rage bubbled up from his gut. Someone had hurt her. Someone had put their hands on her and broken her body.

She looked awful. Bruised, her eyes swollen. One was nearly swollen shut. One of her arms was in a cast and the raised area of the bedding made him think that one of her legs was in a cast as well.

Someone had broken her bones. Three of her fingers were splinted, her hands wrapped in bandages. As was her head.

Her face was the same color as the pillow she lay against.

But her hair was still the same bright red it had been all those years ago. It was dyed now, white roots peeking out, but it had been her natural color then. The bright red made her paleness even more stark.

Beside her was a woman.

Charlotte.

Charlotte sat in a chair, but her arms were folded on the edge of her aunt's bed, her cheek resting on one arm. Mrs. Johnson's free hand was stroking Charlotte's golden-blond hair.

Charlotte's hair color hadn't changed, either.

He couldn't see her face, but there was a box of tissues next to her elbow. Like she'd been crying.

The older woman's eyes were closed, and had it not been for the rhythmic stroking of Charlotte's hair, Tino would have thought she was asleep.

He crept quietly into the room, taking the only other chair and setting it lightly on the other side of the bed, farthest from Charlotte.

"Mrs. Johnson?" he murmured, not wanting to wake Charlotte.

Partly because she seemed exhausted. Partly because he hoped to put off their reunion a little longer.

Until he felt stronger. Because seeing Mrs. Johnson so injured was ripping his heart out.

Slowly Mrs. Johnson turned her head, fixing her open eye on his face. She studied him for a long, long moment—so long that Tino thought that she didn't recognize him.

"I'm Tino—"

"Ciccotelli," she said, her voice hoarse and rasping. "I know who you are." One side of her mouth lifted before she winced. Her lip had been split open, two stitches visible. "Dammit."

Startled, Tino chuckled. "I've never heard you swear before."

"Because you couldn't hear what I was saying in my head when you were in my classroom," she said tartly. Then she saw the sketchbook in his hand. "You're the police artist?"

"I am. If that's okay."

"Of course it is. I've always wondered what happened to you."

"What did you think had happened?"

"That you were in jail," she said dryly. "You and that Cliff Gargano. Always getting into scrapes."

"Never illegal ones, though. Mostly," he amended when she just looked at him. He sighed. "I should have come to visit you."

"Probably. But I get why you didn't. It was awkward."

"I guess that's one word for it." Heart-wrenching was another. To visit her, either at school or at her home, when all it did was bring back memories of Charlotte? "I'm here now, though. And I'm mad as hell at whoever did this to you."

She grimaced. "So am I. So I guess we should get started so that you can be on your way. I'm sure you have other responsibilities."

"Not today. I have all the time in the world for you."

"Well, I don't have all the time in the world before my next pain pill, so..."

He chuckled again. "I missed you."

Another attempt at a smile was followed by another wince. "And I you. You've done well for yourself?"

"I make a living. Mostly work for cops and PIs, but I do portraits occasionally. I own a house with my brother Gino out in Mount Airy. We do okay."

"A bachelor pad."

"Less than you'd think. We clean and everything." He

opened his sketchbook. "So. Let's get started so you can have another pain pill. And don't worry. Now that I know you're here, I'm going to be here every day. You'll get better and be discharged just to be rid of me."

"You're still cheeky."

"Some things don't change."

Mrs. Johnson glanced down at her niece. "Some things do. Should I tell her you were here if she doesn't wake up before you're gone?"

"Yes." *I think.* "Of course. I hope she's been happy."

Mrs. Johnson hesitated. "I don't know. She feels guilty about what happened to me and I don't know why."

Tino frowned. "Guilty how? Like because she wasn't there at the time?"

"I don't know. You should ask her."

"Oh, don't worry. I will. Now, what can you remember about the man who hurt you?"

"He was tall," she began. "Bald. Big fists. Brown eyes. Like amber."

Tino began to sketch.

* * *

PHILADELPHIA, PENNSYLVANIA
TUESDAY, MARCH 29, 10:40 A.M.

"HE WAS TALL. Bald. Big fists. Brown eyes. Like amber."

Charlotte Walsh blinked at the sound of her aunt's voice, wincing as her head throbbed and her neck ached.

She'd started to lift her head when it all came rushing back.

Dottie. Aunt Dottie was here, in the hospital. In the ICU. Because someone had beaten her almost to death.

Charlotte had found her, had thought her dead, even after

she'd checked for a pulse. Dottie's had been so weak that Charlotte had missed it. The medics had arrived quickly, had been so kind.

They'd found a pulse, and Charlotte had found a little hope.

"About how tall, Mrs. J?" a man asked.

He had a nice voice, Charlotte thought. Melodious and deep. Soothing and peaceful. Familiar, but she couldn't place it.

"Six feet," Dottie rasped. "Maybe a little shorter. Average. I'm sorry."

"Hush now," the man said gently. "You don't ever apologize. Never to me. What about his nose?"

Charlotte straightened from where she'd fallen asleep, closing her eyes and swallowing a groan as pain spiked up the back of her neck. It was a usual pain, one that she'd felt several times a day in the years since her car accident, but it never failed to startle her.

A gnarled hand covered hers as the conversation paused.

"Charlie?" Dottie asked. "You okay? You need some ibuprofen?"

That her aunt would be worrying about Charlotte when she was the one in an ICU bed was classic Dottie.

Charlotte forced her lips to curve. Forced her eyes to open so that she could meet Dottie's concerned gaze. "I'm fine." She turned to the man sitting on the other side of the bed. "Who's—"

Her throat closed so abruptly that, for a moment, she couldn't breathe.

His voice had been familiar, and now she knew why.

"Tino," Charlotte whispered.

Tino Ciccotelli. Her first kiss. Her first love.

She'd broken his heart, and for that she'd always hated herself. He hadn't deserved to be treated the way she'd treated him, but she'd been so desperate to break free. So terrified of what he'd offered. So desperate to fly far, far away.

And here I am. Back where I started.

She'd never fly again, her wings permanently clipped.

Broken. I'm broken. And more than a little bitter.

"Charlotte," Tino said quietly, his eyes the same rich dark brown that they'd been when he'd been only fifteen, when he'd first kissed her. Sixteen, when he'd first told her he loved her, his words sweet and uncertain. Seventeen, when he'd said they'd get married and have a house with a white picket fence and meatloaf on Wednesdays.

Eighteen, when his eyes had filled with tears and desperation as he'd begged her to change her mind. To keep him.

To stay.

How she'd turned and walked away from him, she'd never know. But she had.

She'd regretted it ever since.

She hoped he'd found love with someone else, because he deserved it. She hoped he didn't hate her, but she hadn't missed that he'd called her Charlotte when he'd always called her Charlie.

Did you think he'd be glad to see you? No, she couldn't expect that. Even though she may have secretly hoped for it whenever she'd pictured herself seeing him again.

He'd changed, of course. He was older, but still so classically beautiful that it hurt her heart. He'd always reminded her of a Michelangelo sculpture, all those years ago. He still did.

He was broader now, more muscled.

Even more handsome, which didn't seem fair. She was so glad that her scars were covered by her clothing. At least her face looked . . . well, not the same, but she'd aged pretty well. As had he.

His thick, black hair was longer now, almost reaching his shoulders, its natural curl somewhat straightened by the weight of it. He'd worn it short and curly back then. Both styles complemented his face.

Self-consciously, she smoothed her hair as her gaze fell to the sketch pad in his hands. "*You're* the police sketch artist?"

"I am," he said. "Hard to believe, I know."

"*I* thought he'd be in prison," Dottie said dryly.

Charlotte laughed, surprising herself. It had been so long since she'd laughed at anything. "Dottie."

Tino smiled, but it was subdued. "We were working on a description of her attacker, and we're time-constrained. She needs her pain meds."

Charlotte bit back a flinch, his words feeling like a reproach. "I'm sorry, Dottie. I'll be quiet."

Dottie patted her hand. "Nonsense. I'm okay. I can do this." She drew a shallow breath that rattled alarmingly. "Let's go on, Tino."

Charlotte frowned at the rattling sound. All Dottie needed was to get a respiratory infection on top of everything else. Carefully she squeezed her aunt's hand. "I'm going to talk to the nurse, okay? I'll be back soon."

"I'm fine, Charlie."

"I don't like the way you're breathing. I'll be back." She pressed a kiss to Dottie's weathered cheek. "Excuse me, Tino."

She didn't need to hear her aunt describe her attacker again. She'd already heard it several times, as Dottie had been forced to tell her story over and over.

And every time Charlotte had heard it, she'd been secretly, overwhelmingly terrified that the description could be *his*.

It could *have been him*, the little voice in her head insisted. He'd been average height and he'd had big hands. Cruel hands.

Hands that had left her with scars on the inside and outside.

No. It could not *be him.* He'd been in prison for a year and would be for seven more.

She grabbed the cane that rested up against the wall behind Dottie's bed, ignoring Tino's widening eyes as she used it to stand. She didn't always need the cane, but when she was tired she did.

She was so damn tired.

She hoped that she'd managed to keep her expression bland. She wasn't ashamed of the cane, but she didn't want him to see how much it hurt to simply stand.

She still had a little pride, it seemed.

He said nothing, but she could feel his eyes on her as she made her way to the door and out into the hall. But he didn't ask Dottie about her, merely continuing his interview.

"Let's go back to his face," he said to Dottie. "His nose, what was the shape?"

Charlotte heard her aunt telling Tino that the man had a large nose. Dottie remembered his nostrils flaring as he'd hit her. The man had smiled, and it had made him look insane.

It isn't him. He's in prison.

Charlotte had not brought this trouble to her aunt's door. *I'd never forgive myself.*

She found the nurse at the station. "Hi. I'm so sorry to bother you, but my aunt's breathing is labored, and she sounds like she's got an infection or something in her lungs."

"Her nurse heard the same thing," the nurse said kindly. "Her doctor's put her on an antibiotic, and we've called in a respiratory therapist who can hopefully help." The woman tilted her head, studying Charlotte's face. "Do you not remember me?"

Charlotte blinked hard. She'd been sleeping by Dottie's bedside for two days. Everything was fuzzy.

She hadn't recognized the nurse, but now she looked harder, dropping her gaze to the woman's nametag. Marian. *Oh my God.*

This day was becoming one big blast from the past. "*Mrs. Gargano?*"

Mrs. Gargano smiled. "Yes."

Charlotte's cheeks heated. "I'm sorry. I should have recognized you right away." She'd spent a large part of her youth in the Gargano household. Tino and Cliff Gargano had been best friends and Tino had been unhappy at home, so the Gargano house was where they'd all hung out.

"Well, it *has* been twenty years," Mrs. Gargano said, excusing Charlotte's rudeness.

Twenty-four, Charlotte thought, *but who's counting?* "Still. You were so kind to me back then. So good to Tino."

"You were both good kids. It was a pleasure having you both in my home. Tino's still part of our lives, of course. He and Cliff are still best friends and he's godfather to my granddaughter. Cliff and Sonya's baby is only ten months old. They tried for years to get pregnant and had given up long ago. Then . . . well, miracles happen." She patted Charlotte's hand. "Remember that, honey."

"Miracles like my aunt recovering? If she gets pneumonia, that's not good at all."

"No, but we'll work hard to keep it from getting that bad. Can I ask you a personal question?"

Charlotte stiffened. "You can ask."

"The cane. Hip or leg?"

"Both."

"Sleeping in that plastic chair can't be good for it. I'll have a better chair brought in so you can get some rest."

Charlotte waited for more questions. *What happened to your hip and leg? How did it happen? Who did it? What did you do to provoke him?*

But no more questions were asked, and after a moment, her shoulders relaxed. "Thank you, Mrs. Gargano."

She winked. "You can call me Marian now. I'd say you're of age."

I feel ancient. But Charlotte made herself smile. "Marian. You're still very kind." She looked over her shoulder to the room her aunt occupied. The need to know about Tino Ciccotelli's life warred with her unwillingness to seem too curious. Need to know won out. "I didn't expect Tino to become a police artist."

Marian chuckled. "Me either. Tino's been doing work for the police for . . . my goodness. It's been nine years. Started doing some sketches for his brother Vito, who's Homicide."

Charlotte stared. "Vito Ciccotelli is a cop?"

"An important one. Solved a serial killer case nine years ago with some help from Tino's sketches. Maybe you read about it? The killer's name was Simon Vartanian."

The name was familiar and the details she remembered sent a chill down her spine. "I think I read about it in the news. I didn't know Vito and Tino were involved."

"Well, they were. Both of their careers kind of took off then. Tino travels all over the country doing sketches for police departments and private investigators. He's got a real gift." Her eyes widened. "And here he is."

Charlotte turned to see Tino approaching, sketchbook under one arm. "Mrs. Johnson gave me a little information," he said, "but not enough for a decent sketch. I'll come back in a few hours for more. Her pain is just too great right now. She wasn't able to speak toward the end of our interview. She needs her meds."

"I'll see that it happens," Marian promised. "Charlotte, why don't you get something to eat? You've been in your aunt's room for two days and the night nurse said you didn't leave to eat."

Tino turned to frown at Charlotte. "You need to eat. Come on. I'm starving too. We'll get an early lunch." He leaned over the desk to kiss Marian's cheek. "See you later, Mrs. G." He took Charlotte's arm, gently steering her toward the elevator.

"I can't just leave Dottie," Charlotte protested, pulling her arm free.

Tino released his hold immediately. "She wanted you to take care of yourself. That was the last thing she told me before the pain took over. She knows you haven't left her side, and she's worried. Let's go eat, and I'll bring you right back. We won't even go far. I promise."

Charlotte looked back at the nurses' desk. Marian was speaking to Dottie's nurse and the two of them looked up, both giving her shooing motions.

"Fine," she grumbled. "But just fast food. I can't take too much time."

Tino scoffed. "I thought you became a chef."

"I did. And how did you know that?"

Tino had the grace to look a bit abashed. "I looked you up once, years ago."

"Well, I'm not a chef anymore, and I need to eat quickly."

Tino pressed the button for the elevator. "I know just the place."

CHAPTER 2

Mrs. Johnson had tried to describe her attacker. She'd really tried. But she'd been far more worried about her niece and her mind had wandered. And then she'd been overcome by the pain, her words becoming slurred, her thoughts fragmented.

Tino had seen it so many times before. He'd learned to listen to what the victims said because they often buried snippets of the description of their attacker in what seemed, on the surface, to be random conversation.

It was their way of coping. All he had to do was be patient and whoever he was interviewing would usually come around to the point. Mrs. Johnson would, too, but it might happen faster if she were no longer worried about Charlotte.

Charlotte, who leaned on a cane, pain tightening her features. She'd tried to hide it, but Tino was a trained observer. He hadn't missed the twinges, the winces. The lifting of her chin as she walked beside him.

He'd already slowed his pace so that she wouldn't have to

race to keep up. She was five-six to his five-eleven. When they'd been kids, she'd been full of bounce and vigor, often racing ahead of him before turning back with a teasing smile. *Hurry up, Tino. We're going to be late.*

She'd never been late to anything—except their last dinner together. The dinner where she'd told him that she was going to school in California. All the way across the country. He'd immediately considered how he'd follow her, what kind of job he could get. How he could leave his parents. His brothers and sister.

But he hadn't needed to do that. She'd been adamant that they were over, that she was going to chase her dreams. He'd been heartbroken, watching her walk away from him.

He wondered now what had happened to Charlotte's dreams. She said she wasn't a chef anymore and he needed to know why. But he recognized the set to her jaw. She was stubborn, so he'd have to be as patient with her as he was with the victims he interviewed.

"Here we are," he said, stopping at the door of Burt & Angela's. "This place is in my top five favorite restaurants in the city."

Charlotte lifted her brows. "That's saying a lot. Philly's got some of the best restaurants in the country. I don't remember this place."

"I only discovered it a few years ago. I do a lot of work with victims and their families at the hospital. One of the nurses brought back a meatball sandwich from this place and she shared it with me. I was instantly in love."

"With the nurse?"

Tino chuckled. "With the sandwich. The nurse was flirting, but she wasn't for me. Nice woman, just . . . not for me." He opened the door for Charlotte. "After you."

She entered, looking around with interest. It was a diner

with old booths, many of which were held together with duct tape. The walls were covered in posters of magical destinations —Paris, Athens, Rio. But Charlotte wasn't looking at the booths or the walls. She was staring at the big window into the kitchen, watching as the food was prepared.

"This is going to be delicious," she said.

"It definitely will."

"Tino!" Angela came out of the kitchen, a huge smile on her face. "It's been too long since we've seen you."

Tino opened his arms and enveloped Angela in a bear hug. "It's been two weeks."

"Like I said, too long." She patted his face as she stepped back, giving Charlotte an interested look, head to toe. "And who do we have here?"

"My friend Charlotte. Her aunt's in the hospital and she's been sitting at her bedside. She needs to be fed."

"Ah. Taking care of others before herself. We *will* feed her." She grabbed a menu and gestured for them to follow. "This way." She seated them in the back of the restaurant where it was quieter. "You can chat without all the noise." She placed the menu in front of Charlotte. "I hope your aunt recovers, honey."

Charlotte's smile was small but genuine. "Thank you."

Angela patted Tino's shoulder. "This one will take good care of you."

Charlotte met Tino's gaze. "I know."

Tino waited until Angela had bustled off to take care of another customer then folded his hands on the table. "Everything on the menu is good."

Charlotte frowned. "She didn't give you a menu."

"Because I've memorized it. I've tried everything on it, but I usually get the eggplant parmigiana if I'm eating here. I get the meatball sandwich if I'm taking it home."

"Where is home?"

"Mount Airy. My brother Gino and I bought a house out there."

One side of her mouth lifted. "Bachelor pad."

He rolled his eyes. "Everyone always says that, but we keep it tidy. We even have a housekeeper come in every two weeks."

Her lips twitched. "But there *is* a man cave in the basement?"

He grinned. "With a big-ass flat-screen for football and a full bar. Homemade brew on tap."

"Who makes the beer?"

"I do. I get gaps between jobs, and brewing beer keeps me busy. That and babysitting my nieces and nephews. Dino has five kids and Vito has two with one on the way."

Her expression became wistful. "That must be nice."

You could have had that, Tino wanted to say. *You could have had me.*

But he kept those thoughts to himself, curious as to what had become of her. Curious as to why she was no longer a chef. Curious as to why she used a cane. Curious as to why her aunt thought she felt guilty for the attack. But he kept those questions to himself as well.

"No husband or kids?" he asked instead.

She shook her head with a slight grimace. "Divorced. Messy. You?"

That she was single shouldn't have made him so happy. But it did. She'd aged, sure, but she was still the prettiest woman he'd ever known. Her hair was still golden, her eyes still the same blue.

His body still responded to her. Still wanted her.

Which was stupid. But it was true.

He pushed the desire away, focusing on the question she'd asked.

It should have felt awkward, talking after so many years apart. Especially after the way they'd parted. But it didn't. It felt . . . familiar. "Engaged once. Broke it off. We were better friends than life partners."

She nodded once, but her eyes flickered with what might have been satisfaction.

He wasn't going to let his mind go there. He was here to give her comfort and support. Maybe to find out why she felt guilty for her aunt's assault. Not to fall back into old habits.

She'd been a habit, he'd told himself over and over after she'd left. Not his lover. Not his partner. Just a habit.

It sounded as false now as it had twenty-four years ago.

He was a forty-two-year-old man who traveled for a living. When he came home, it was to the house he shared with his brother.

If she hadn't thought him worth staying for when he'd been eighteen, when life had been full of possibilities . . . Well, he wasn't going to wonder about what might have been. What could still be.

This was a meeting due to circumstance.

And the circumstance was a tragic one.

"You're still friends with Cliff Gargano," she commented. "His mother said so."

"Still thick as thieves. We're both boring old men now, though," he added ruefully. "He's a daddy. Finally. Their little girl is so frickin' cute." He pulled out his phone, easily finding a photo of little Addison. His phone was full of them.

Charlotte smiled. "She looks like Sonya. She's their little miracle, Mrs. Gargano said."

"Truth." He set his phone aside and decided to take the plunge into what he really needed to know. "Your aunt is worried about you."

"I know. She always has been."

"She thinks you feel guilty for what happened to her, and she's not sure why."

Charlotte flinched. "Well, that's blunt."

Tino shrugged. "We don't have much time. I need to get you back to the hospital, and I promised her I'd try to help you."

Charlotte swallowed hard. "It's . . ." She trailed off, shaking her head. "It's personal and not related to what happened to Dottie."

"Okay," he said simply. He'd let it go for now, but he would follow up later because he didn't think that Charlotte entirely believed her own words. There was doubt in her eyes, a tremble in her voice. "Here's Angela. Did you decide what you want to eat?"

She looked up at Angela, who'd stopped at their table with an expectant smile. "I'll try the meatball sandwich, please. I've heard it's wonderful."

Angela beamed. "It is. My Burt is the very best chef in the city. Tino? The usual?"

"Make it two sandwiches. We need to be getting back to the hospital soon, so we may end up taking some of it to go."

"I'll make it quick," Angela promised, then hustled back to the kitchen, shouting their order.

Charlotte was regarding him with a pensive expression.

"What?" he asked. "I like the meatball sandwich, too."

She shook her head. "You're not going to press me for details?"

"Maybe later. Not now."

"That's what I figured." She sighed. "You can find it if you google it."

"Find what?"

"The report about my . . ." She sighed again. "My assault."

He stared at her, shocked. Was that why she now used a cane? Someone had hurt her? *Who do I need to kill?* "What assault?"

"A man back in Memphis. That's where I lived for, gosh—

fifteen years now. My ex's family lives there so when we got married, we moved there. After the divorce, I just stayed. My business was there."

"But not your chef business."

"At the beginning, yes. I was the head chef in a very nice restaurant in Memphis for about four years. Then my ex and I were in a car accident." She lifted the cane. "Broke my pelvis. I did all the physical therapy and managed to eventually return to my job, but I couldn't manage the hours on my feet anymore. So I had to give it up."

He wanted to say he was sorry, but he sensed she didn't want that. "What did you do instead?"

"Became a restaurant critic."

His brows shot up. "I wasn't expecting that."

"Not many people do. Long story short, my column became popular and I became locally notorious. I didn't write under my own name and I wore disguises every time I was working. Never took the cane, as that would have been a memorable detail. I wanted to be incognito. No special treatment."

"You wanted to experience the food the way a normal person would." He winced. "A person who wasn't a food critic."

"I knew what you meant, and yes. That's why I did it. Turns out that anonymity kept me safe for a long time. Then a year ago a restaurant owner had to declare bankruptcy and blamed my review."

"Not five stars, I take it."

"Not even one. The place was filthy, the food was frozen, cooked in a microwave. The servers were untrained and rude. One of them hit on me, then called me a bitch when I turned him down."

"Wow."

"Yeah. So the health department went in and found a ton of violations. My review didn't shut the place down. His own negligence did. But he wasn't just negligent. He was mentally ill and unraveling—and it showed up in his cooking and every other aspect of his restaurant."

"He came after you."

"He did. Took him months to figure out who I was."

"How did he?"

"Bribed someone at the newspaper where I worked to give him tax info. Showed my real name and address. He was waiting for me when I got home one night, about a year ago." She closed her eyes. "It wasn't pretty."

Tino reached across the table and covered her hand with his. "Where is he now?"

Her eyes opened, her gaze dropping to their hands. "Prison. He was sentenced to eight years."

"Not enough."

"No. But I always wonder now if someone is following me. If someone is stalking me. And when I found Dottie lying in a pool of her own blood, I had to wonder if it was my fault. The man who attacked me was average in height with big hands. But there are a lot of men of average height with big hands, so it's just me being paranoid again. I call it being hypervigilant, but I know I'm really just being paranoid. I can't help it. I think I see him—or someone like him—every time I turn around. I think he's hiding in the shadows. Behind a tree." She made a face, looking embarrassed at the admission. "My therapist says to cut myself some slack, that it will be better soon."

He kept his expression calm. He'd had a lot of practice over the years, staying calm while talking to victims or witnesses. But this wasn't just any victim. This was Charlotte.

"I have to agree with your therapist. But your aunt's assault can't have been connected to yours. Your Memphis attacker is in prison." Then he understood her fear about ongoing stalkers. "You're still doing restaurant reviews?"

"I am. I'm more careful now and I've gone freelance. No one has access to my address and pay records other than the IRS. I even do my own accounting and tax prep."

"I don't blame you. Are you using the name you used before?"

"I am. I almost didn't, but I couldn't start all over again."

"I get that," he said gently, because she'd said it so apologetically. "You have to make a living."

She nodded, looking relieved. "So now you know my big secret. You can tell Aunt Dottie that it's just misplaced guilt because I wasn't with her at the time."

Tino managed not to shudder, but it was close. "If you'd been home, he might have hurt you, too."

Her chin lifted. "Better me than a seventy-five-year-old woman who can't defend herself."

"Better that nobody gets hurt. But I get your point of view. You know how to defend yourself?"

"Now I do. I took classes targeted at people with disabilities."

"Smart." He smiled at her, shoving away his own roiling feelings of rage. Someone had put his hands on her, had hurt her. Had made her afraid. "Are you here in Philly permanently?"

Her expression tightened. "Yeah. Couldn't stay in Memphis. Too many bad memories."

He frowned, thinking things through. "But if you are reviewing Philly restaurants under your old moniker, then someone will know where to find you."

She shook her head. "I take the train to New York or Baltimore. Do reviews there."

That made him feel better—except it meant she was alone on trains.

Lots of women travel alone on trains and they're fine.

But he wasn't thinking about lots of women. He was thinking about Charlotte.

"Does your aunt know? About the assault?"

"No. I didn't want her to worry, so I told her that I was just ready to come home. That wasn't a lie."

"Well, now I can tell your aunt that you're okay." Kind of. She was becoming okay, at least. "Thank you for telling me."

Her smile was wry. "Figured you'd poke around until you figured it out. Saved us both some time."

"You did. And here is the best meatball sandwich you'll find in Philly," he said when Angela slid two plates in front of them with two takeaway boxes.

"In case you need to eat and run," she said.

"Thank you, Angela," Charlotte said, drawing in a deep breath. "It smells heavenly." She took a bite and groaned. "Oh my God. This is good."

"Told you," Tino said smugly, telling himself not to react to her groan. He'd heard it before, many times. Sometimes it was because she'd just tasted something wonderful.

Sometimes it was because *he* had tasted something wonderful. *No, no, no.* He was not letting his mind go there.

Angela grinned and left them to their meal.

"I didn't realize how hungry I was," Charlotte said. "Thank you, Tino. For taking care of me today."

He could only nod. He would have gladly taken care of her forever once upon a time. Those days were gone, but he was glad that he could take care of her today.

He cleared his throat, the words exiting his mouth before he knew he'd planned to say them. "Have dinner with me tonight."

Her eyes widened, her jaw freezing mid-chew.

Shut up. Shut up now. Tell her she doesn't have to. That you were just kidding. But those weren't the words that he said.

"I'll show you another one of my favorite restaurants. You can enjoy a meal without having to review it."

She finished chewing the bite she'd taken, then tilted her head, studying him. "Okay."

He was surprised. "Okay?"

She smiled hesitantly. "Okay. We were friends once. We can be again."

Friends. He made himself smile. "Of course we can."

* * *

MOUNT AIRY, PHILADELPHIA, PENNSYLVANIA
TUESDAY, MARCH 29, 1:15 P.M.

"YOU'RE BACK FROM KNOXVILLE," Vito said when he answered Tino's call.

Tino shook the bag of dirty clothes into the washing machine in his basement. He made it a rule to do laundry as soon as he got home from a trip, because if he put it off, it would never get done. "This morning. I got a call about the victim of a beating."

Mrs. Johnson's assault wasn't being investigated by his brother's department. Vito was the lieutenant over Homicide, but he might be able to make some calls on Charlotte's behalf.

Tino wanted to make damn sure that the asshole who'd hurt her was still behind bars.

Vito was quiet for a moment and Tino could hear road noise in the background. Vito must be in the car. "You sound off, T," Vito finally said. "What's going on?"

"What's wrong?" a woman demanded. "Is Tino okay?"

That was Vito's wife, Sophie, one of Tino's favorite people in all the world.

"Tell Sophie that I'm fine. Mostly. A little rattled," he confessed. "The victim is Mrs. Johnson, my old art teacher from high school."

"Oh no," Vito said, sounding both shocked and sad. "I liked her. Is she going to make it?"

"Who?" Sophie demanded louder. "Dammit, Vito, put him on speaker."

Vito, being a very smart man, put the phone on speaker.

"Who are you talking about, Tino?" Sophie asked.

Tino might blame both her bossiness and nosiness on her pregnancy, but she'd always been like that. He loved her so much.

"My case this morning was my old art teacher from high school."

"The one who told you that you were good," Sophie said, her voice softening.

Tino wasn't surprised that she remembered, even though he'd mentioned Mrs. Johnson only once that he could recall. Sophie had a memory like a steel trap and the softest of hearts.

"She's the one." He drew a breath. "Charlotte's here," he blurted out. He wouldn't call her Charlie. Not ever again. He needed to keep her at arm's length. He needed to protect his heart.

"Oh," Vito said, a lot of feeling going into the single word. "Tell me you're not tempted by her. Please tell me this."

"I'm not," Tino said. "I promise."

Liar, liar, pants on fire. He'd been *so* tempted. But he'd held strong. Kept his emotional distance. He sighed silently. *Liar.*

"Good. When does she go back to wherever she came from?"

"Vito!" Sophie admonished. "What the hell is wrong with you?"

"She broke his heart, Soph," Vito said. "Trampled all over it and then walked away. It took him *years* to get over her. I had to help him pick up the pieces, and it broke my heart, too."

Tino wanted to deny it, but it was true, at least the heart-trampling part.

"Oh," Sophie said quietly. "I remember you telling me about her a long time ago. Do I need to threaten her, Tino?"

Tino closed the laundry room door and sank into the leather sofa in his and Gino's basement man cave. "Not necessary, Sophie, but thank you for the kind offer. Charlotte's back in Philly permanently."

"Why?" Vito asked coldly.

"She was hurt. Attacked by a stalker. I don't know how bad her injuries were, but she was hurt badly enough that she didn't want to stay in Memphis any longer."

"Is she worried that the attack on her aunt is connected to her attack?" Sophie asked, always on the ball.

"She is. The guy's in prison—or he's supposed to be. I was hoping you could check on it for me. It would settle her mind."

"I'm taking Sophie to her obstetrician right now. It'll have to wait until I'm back in the office. Both my assistant and my analyst are out sick, and I've put several of my detectives on a string of neighborhood murders so I'm shorthanded right now. Who requested the sketch?"

"Nick Lawrence," Tino said, naming the head of the unit that investigated major crimes and assaults. "Don't worry about this. I'll call Nick."

"Why didn't you call him first?" Vito asked.

"I didn't want to have to explain my background with Charlotte. He's kind of nosy."

Vito chuckled. "He is, but he'll help you. You won't even need to explain why you're asking."

"It's Nick," Tino said flatly, and Vito chuckled again.

"I told him last week to stop matchmaking and he said he would."

"He lied," Sophie said. "He called me two days ago asking for my help in setting Tino up with a nice woman who's just relocated from Albuquerque."

"And you said?" Tino asked, annoyance creeping into his voice. He loved Nick Lawrence like a brother. The man had been Vito's partner in the Homicide Division for years. But he did not care for the continuous matchmaking.

"I told him that you wouldn't like me interfering," Sophie said dutifully.

"And then you said?" Tino asked.

"I said I'd talk to you about it. Which I now have. She does seem like a nice woman from her social media."

"You stalked her socials?" Tino asked, not really shocked.

"Only a little. And you can't be mad at me because I'm pregnant."

Tino laughed. "Goodbye, Sophie. Have fun at the doc's. If you get a new sonogram photo, I want to see it."

"Deal." She hesitated. "Be careful, Tino. With your heart, I mean. I don't want this Charlotte person hurting you again."

"I'm not eighteen anymore," Tino said. "And neither is she. We can be friends."

The words stabbed at his chest, just as they had when she'd said them at the diner over lunch.

Vito sighed. "Do the sketch for the victim and walk away, brother."

"I will. Bye now." He ended the call and leaned his head back into the soft sofa, remembering the haunted look in Charlotte's blue eyes when she'd told him about her attack. She was not okay.

He knew he wouldn't walk away. He couldn't. Not as long as she needed him.

Besides, they were having dinner together tonight. He was very glad he hadn't shared that fact with his brother and Sophie.

Squaring his shoulders, he dialed Nick Lawrence's cell phone.

"Tino! Did you see Mrs. Johnson?"

"Yeah, I did. Did you know that I knew her a long time ago?"

Nick sucked in a startled breath. "I didn't. How?"

"She was my high school art teacher." *Rip off the Band-Aid, Ciccotelli.* "And her niece was my prom date."

Charlotte had been so much more than that, of course. She'd been his everything. *Until she left you. Don't forget that she left you.*

"Well, shit." Nick hadn't lost his southern drawl, even after having lived in Philly for years. He still drew "shit" out to at least three syllables, sometimes four. "Is this going to impact your ability to get a sketch?"

"No. I didn't finish this morning because Mrs. Johnson needed her pain medication, which made her sleep. I'll go back this afternoon and try again. The reason I'm calling is, did you know that her niece was a recent victim of an assault in Memphis?"

"No. I didn't. Neither of them mentioned it. You think it's connected?"

"No, but I want to be sure. The guy who hurt the niece is in prison. Can you verify that he's really still there?"

"Of course. Thanks for the lead. So, Tino, I have—"

"No," Tino said firmly. "If this is about the nice lady from Albuquerque, then no. For the love of all that's holy, *no.*"

Nick made a grumpy sound. "Sophie narced on me."

"She did. Let the matchmaking thing go, Nick," he begged. "Please."

"Fine. Whatever. Just want you to be happy."

He sounded so wounded that Tino had to smile. "I know. I'll be happy if you leave me alone. Let me know what you find out, okay? The niece is Charlotte Walsh. At least that was her last name when I knew her."

He hadn't asked if she'd changed it when she'd gotten married or after the divorce.

"Still is. I'll make some calls. Let me know when you have

that sketch. We got an image of Mrs. Johnson's attacker from a neighbor's security camera, but the guy wore a hoodie and we couldn't see his face. He left no trace of himself behind. That's why we were hoping you could get a sketch. The old lady is the only person who saw him clearly."

"I'll send it over as soon as I'm finished with it," Tino promised. He ended the call and closed his eyes. He'd had an early flight and needed a nap.

CHAPTER 3

DAMMIT. Dottie's little window garden was destroyed.

Charlotte stood in front of her aunt's rowhouse, staring in dismay at the mangled window box. Last week it had been filled with at least five different kinds of daffodils, with impatiens and sweet peas mixed in. It was a delicate cacophony of color, and Dottie had been so proud of it.

Now, it was ruined. The flowers had been ripped out and lay strewn on the ground.

Who would have done such a thing? Dottie had suffered enough without this.

Charlotte pulled out her phone and snapped a photo of the mess. She wasn't sure who she'd show it to or what they might do about it. But if the cops had done this when they were processing the crime scene, she was going to have words with them. This mess was inexcusable.

She'd worked herself up a head of angry steam when the

sound of a closing door had her whipping her gaze to the right, her heart leaping into her throat.

Her aunt had been viciously beaten here in her home where she should have been safe. It had triggered Charlotte's memories of her own attack. Also in her home. Also where she should have been safe.

It can't be him. He's in prison.

Please let him still be in prison.

Please, please, please.

It took a moment for her panic to subside, for her to see the woman standing on the stoop next door.

"Mrs. Murphy." Aunt Dottie's best friend and sometimes nemesis—but only when it came to flowers. The two had been neighbors for more than forty years and kept their window box competition in the friendly zone. Mostly.

Mrs. Murphy was frowning, her concern clear. "Charlie, child, are you all right?"

"Yes," Charlotte said, forcing a smile that felt as fake as it was. "What happened to Dottie's flowers? Did the cops do this?"

"Oh no. Not the cops." Mrs. Murphy slowly shuffled sideways down her front stairs using her walker, her arthritis visibly worse than it had been just last week. She was in an obvious flare-up.

Charlotte knew just the food she'd make for her aunt's best friend. She had a recipe for a fish dish that had all kinds of good anti-inflammatory properties. And berries for dessert. Berries were also good for reducing inflammation, and she knew dozens of ways to prepare them. Hundreds of ways.

She was no longer a professional chef, but she still loved to cook.

Maybe she could cook for Tino.

And ... *no.* She was not even considering it.

But you're friends again. Friends cook for friends. If she cooked for him, maybe he'd call her Charlie again.

No, she thought firmly. *Not gonna happen.* It was cruel to Tino for her to expect it and cruel to herself to hope for it. They'd be friends. Nothing more.

She brought her mind back to the conversation at hand, shoving Tino Ciccotelli out of her thoughts. She had a lot of practice doing so. She'd been shoving Tino out of her thoughts since the day she'd walked away from him.

"If it wasn't the cops, then who did this?" Charlotte gestured to the ruined window box. "Was it those teenagers from up the block?"

"No, it wasn't the kids. I don't know who it was, but I saw him." Mrs. Murphy finally reached her side and scowled at the flowers on the ground.

Charlotte froze. "Him?"

The older woman met her gaze. "It was a man wearing a gray hoodie. Didn't see his face. He was trying to break the window, trying to get inside the house, I guess. My son put a stronger lock on the doors and windows after Dottie was . . ." She swallowed audibly. "After she was hurt. Put stronger locks on my doors and windows, too."

Charlotte opened her mouth, but no words came out.

Mrs. Murphy grabbed her arm, squeezing hard. "Charlie."

Charlotte blinked and Mrs. Murphy's face came back into focus. How long she'd been staring blankly, she didn't know.

Mrs. Murphy searched her face. "Okay, you're back. Do you get panic attacks?"

"Recently, yes." Since her assault a year ago, but she wasn't going to admit that. Not to Mrs. Murphy. Her aunt would be informed before the hour was out. "I'm sorry."

Mrs. Murphy gave her a don't-be-stupid look. "Come with me. I'll make some tea."

Charlotte shook her head, her heart beating like a hummingbird's wings. "I was going to get Dottie's robe and slippers and the book she was reading. I'm going to read to her. She'll want her things."

She was babbling and couldn't seem to stop.

Mrs. Murphy squeezed her arm again, the old woman's grip almost painful. "Charlie. Stop. Listen to me. You're still panicking. Come with me and we'll figure this out." She tugged on Charlotte's arm, somehow steering them both up the stairs while hunched over her walker.

Charlotte let herself be dragged into Mrs. Murphy's kitchen and lowered herself into the chair, wincing when her hip protested the solid wood seat. She'd left her cane in her car, still parked on the curb in front of Dottie's house. She'd thought that she would only be a minute and that she'd use her aunt's stair lift to get up to Dottie's bedroom. Then all rational thought had fled when she'd seen the mess.

A steaming cup of green tea was placed in front of her, Mrs. Murphy grimacing as she, too, sat down. "Drink," the woman commanded.

So Charlotte sipped, feeling herself calm a little. Just a little, though.

He'd returned. The man who'd hurt Dottie. The man who'd left her aunt for dead.

Or . . . it could have been someone else. "Could it have been a curious person? Someone who wanted to see the scene of a crime?"

"It's possible. I turned on my front-porch light and he froze, like a deer in the headlights. I have a superbright light now. My son just installed it after Dottie . . ." She shook her head. "I didn't say anything to the man." The words sounded like a confession. "I'm sorry, Charlie. I was too scared to confront him."

"No, no. Don't be sorry. You were smart not to confront him.

If it was the same man, he could have hurt you, too. What happened when you turned on the light?"

"He spun around to face me, both hands filled with daffodils. We kind of stared at each other for a minute, then he threw the flowers on the ground and took off toward the avenue."

Passyunk Avenue was a major artery through the neighborhood. Lots of stores and restaurants. "Maybe a security camera got his face." Then she frowned. "If you stared at each other, did you see his face? Maybe a little of it?"

Mrs. Murphy blinked. "I guess I did. It wasn't a full view and he had a mask on. One of those . . . what do you call them? They're a knitted tube and you wear it around your neck but can pull it up over your face."

"A neck gaiter?"

Mrs. Murphy nodded hard. "Yes. A gaiter. It was . . ." She frowned, thinking. "Orange. Orange and black."

Philadelphia Flyers colors, Charlotte thought, wondering if the man was a hockey fan. And wondering why he'd wear something so bright to break into a woman's home.

Charlotte's attacker had been dressed all in black. "Did you see his eyes?"

"I must have." The older woman frowned. "I did. But only his eyes."

Charlotte thought about Tino. "A police sketch artist visited Dottie in the hospital this morning. Could you talk to him? Maybe help him with the eyes?"

Mrs. Murphy hesitated, but only for a heartbeat. "Yes. Do you think he can come here?"

"I think he would. The artist was one of Dottie's students a long time ago. He wants her attacker caught."

"Good."

"Did you call the police?"

"Of course I did," Mrs. Murphy said, her tone going a little bit haughty. "I called my son first and he rushed over, but the police came out. Took some fingerprints, but the man wore gloves, so they're not going to get anything. They asked me to leave the flowers where they were. That they'd send someone out to take photos."

"Did they?"

"Not yet, but I bet you could light a fire under their asses better than I can. My son unlocked Dottie's door so that one of the officers could look around. Nobody was inside. My son locked it back up. I made you a key. If it's all right with you, we'll keep a copy, too."

Charlotte found a genuine smile. "Of course that's all right. You've had a key to Dottie's house for how long?"

"Since before you were born," Mrs. Murphy said. "Your color is better. I thought you were going to pass out on me."

"I might have. Thank you, Mrs. Murphy."

Mrs. Murphy's smile was sad. "You're welcome. I wish things were different, that Dottie was in her house and fussing at me for having nicer flowers this year. She'd be wrong, though. Hers were stunning." A tear streaked down her wrinkled cheek. "Always better than mine. But that's to remain a secret. Just between us."

Charlotte carefully covered the woman's gnarled hand with her own. "Just between us. You grabbed me pretty hard. That must have hurt your hand."

"Needed to be done. Or I could have slapped you like they do in the movies."

Charlotte chuckled, surprising herself. "Don't do that. I was so out of it that I might have slapped you back, just out of reflex."

Mrs. Murphy laughed quietly. "Then think of how awful you would have felt. I might have even taken advantage of your guilt to get some cream puffs."

"I'll make you some. Along with something to help with the flare-up."

"That berry dessert was wonderful."

"It's on my list to make for you."

"You're a good girl," Mrs. Murphy said fondly.

I wish I were still a girl. Charlotte thought of Tino once again. *I'd do so many things differently.*

Mrs. Murphy was watching her, eyes sharp. "You can talk to me, you know. If you're not okay."

"Thank you, ma'am. But I'll be fine." *I always am.* "This tea is good."

"And you're just as bad at changing the subject as Dottie. Drink it. It's good for you. Antioxidants or some such thing."

Charlotte obeyed, and when they were both finished, she washed their mugs and put them in the dish drainer. She was calmer now. Able to think. "I wonder why he came back. If it was the same guy."

Mrs. Murphy shrugged. "I don't know. My son and I racked our brains over it and came up with nothing. We thought maybe he was afraid she could identify him and came back to . . . you know. Finish her." They both winced at that thought. "But my son said that Dottie's assault has been in the news and all the reports say she's in critical condition in the hospital. Whoever hurt her wouldn't have come back to finish her off, because everyone knows she's not home."

"Maybe it wasn't her attacker, just some guy in a gray hoodie. Some opportunistic jerk who knew she wasn't home and thought he'd steal from her."

"But Dottie doesn't have anything valuable. Nothing anyone would want to steal."

"He wouldn't have known that."

"Well, he'll think twice before coming back. My son put cameras up when he fixed the locks, but this morning he installed even better cameras. If that bastard comes back, we will get his photo."

"I hope he doesn't come back. I have faith in your son's abilities, but I'd prefer not to test them out." She took a step, gritting her teeth when her hip joints protested.

I'm going to double the berry recipe. I need to eat some anti-inflammatory foods myself.

But she was going out to dinner tonight. With Tino Ciccotelli.

She'd cook tomorrow. She had a list of people to cook for anyway. She'd made a few friends since returning to Philly, and those friends had been through their own recent trauma. Cooking for them was the only way she knew to help.

"Thank you for the tea, Mrs. Murphy. I'll call you when I've talked to the police sketch artist."

"All right. You'll call? With your voice? None of that texting nonsense?"

Charlotte nodded soberly, keeping her lips from twitching. "I promise. Now, I need to go over and get Dottie's slippers and robe."

"And the book you're going to read to her." Mrs. Murphy's eyes lit up with an unholy glee. "I'd love to be a fly on her hospital room wall."

Charlotte narrowed her eyes. "Why?"

"She's reading a romance. A steamy one. She'll probably want you to skip to the really juicy parts."

Charlotte laughed. "If that's what she wants, that's what I'll do."

* * *

PHILADELPHIA, PENNSYLVANIA
TUESDAY, MARCH 29, 6:55 P.M.

TINO PUSHED AWAY from the wall he'd been leaning on when
Charlotte got out of the Uber in front of the restaurant. He'd
been afraid she wouldn't come, but here she was, looking as
tentative as he felt.

This was probably a bad idea, seeing her again like this. He
could have kept things casual. Professional even. He could have
treated her as he did every family member of every victim or
witness he'd interviewed for a sketch.

He could have simply said goodbye and wished her a nice
life when he'd seen her at the hospital once again that afternoon
after finishing his interview with Mrs. Johnson.

He could have told Charlotte that he was busy tonight, that
something had come up. He could have canceled this dinner.

But he hadn't done any of those things because she'd looked
so damn frightened and vulnerable. Someone had tried to break
into her aunt's house during the night, destroying Mrs. J's flower
beds in an apparent rage because he couldn't pry the window
open.

That Philly PD hadn't informed her as Mrs. J's next of kin
was something he'd given Nick Lawrence a ration of shit about.
Nick had agreed with him, calling Charlotte with a personal
apology. Yes, Philly PD was busy, but they'd owed her a
heads up.

Nick had also told her that he was checking on her attacker
back in Memphis but hadn't yet heard back from the prison
where the man was serving his sentence.

The gratitude in Charlotte's eyes when she'd realized that
Tino had gone to bat for her with the Philly PD had been like a
physical punch to the gut. She'd been dealing with too many
things all alone.

Tino could help with some of those things. Because that's what friends did for one another, and they were friends. Or they had been.

Hopefully they would be again.

She paused at the curb, looking around warily before approaching him. "I thought you'd be inside already," she said.

"I confirmed our reservation," he said, "then came out here to wait."

Her lips quirked. "You thought I might not show up."

He shrugged. "It crossed my mind."

"I wouldn't do that to you." She looked over her shoulder again with a slight frown. "Let's go inside. It's chilly tonight."

He took her arm, leading her to the door. "What's wrong?"

"Nothing. Just jumpy. I see shadows and it freaks me out. Just me being paranoid."

"I don't blame you, especially after the attempted break-in last night. I'm glad you weren't there." It had been a small comfort, knowing that she'd been safe in Mrs. J's hospital room all night. But she couldn't stay there forever. "Where are you going to stay tonight?"

"My apartment, I think. Marian Gargano was so nice to get me a more comfortable chair, but my bones are telling me to sleep in a bed tonight, and I'll be sorry if I don't listen to my bones. The nurses said they'd call me if Dottie has any problems during the night. I'm a light sleeper, so the phone will wake me up."

Tino didn't want her alone in her apartment, but she lifted her chin, as if challenging him to try arguing. He wisely kept his words to himself as he followed Charlotte into the restaurant.

"We're ready now," Tino said to the woman behind the podium.

The woman grinned at him. "Prepare yourself. Polina is here tonight. You're going to get hugged."

Charlotte's brows rose as they followed the woman to their table. "Who is Polina, and why will she hug you?"

That she sounded a little miffed was good for Tino's ego. "She's the owner of the restaurant. My brother Gino's company built this place and I did some of the artwork. Polina was so happy with the result that she kind of adopted us."

"Many women seem to have adopted you," Charlotte said dryly. "Marian Gargano, Angela from this morning, and now this Polina."

Tino laughed. "I'm not complaining. Most of them feed me."

He pulled out Charlotte's chair for her, more out of habit than anything else. She'd insisted on it when they'd been teenagers. She'd said her mother taught her not to date boys who didn't have manners.

In the many years that had followed, Tino had rarely pulled out a chair for another woman without remembering Charlotte.

"What?" she asked softly when he'd taken his own seat. "Your face just got sad."

"Memories," he said, hoping she'd leave it alone.

"Yeah," she murmured. "Having a lot of those today. But artwork." She looked around. "They're all portraits. Which ones did you do?"

"All of them," Tino said. "Polina especially likes the one I did of her and her husband. Her parents and grandparents, too." He pointed to the far wall where the six portraits hung. "She wanted a wall where she could showcase her family, since the recipes she uses were passed down from her grandparents."

Charlotte studied the portraits for a long moment before she smiled. "You do faces so well. What other portraits have you painted?"

Tino felt his cheeks heat. "Well, for a while I was doing more . . . personal portraits. Mostly married women who wanted something sexy to give to their husbands."

She laughed, the sound husky and inviting. "You did boudoir portraits?"

Her laughter took him back once again. Made him want what he couldn't have. "Don't knock the boudoir portraits. They helped me earn my half of the down payment on the house my brother Gino and I own. We bought the house intending to flip it, but we liked it too much to part with it once we were done. So we kept it."

Her expression sobered. "You always wanted a house of your own. Does it have a white picket fence?"

He had to take a deep breath. He'd grieved the loss of the married life he'd envisioned after she'd left for college. She clearly hadn't shared his dream, being so very desperate to leave Philly, to leave everything behind and have adventure. That was what she'd called it then. Adventure.

"It does. I finally realized I could have my dream house even if I was alone."

She winced and he considered retracting the words or at least apologizing, but if they were to move forward, even as friends, he had to be honest.

"I'm glad you have it," she said stiffly, then sighed. "And I deserved that."

"You didn't, but I deserved to be able to say it."

"That's fair." She picked up her menu. "What's good here?"

"Everything, but my favorite is the spanakopita. Save room for dessert. Polina makes a baklava that's to—" He cut himself off before he could say *to die for.* "It's like nothing you've ever tasted."

"You can say 'to die for,'" she said, smirking slightly. "My stalker didn't actually kill me, after all."

Tino shuddered. "Thank God for that."

"I do." She put her menu aside and folded her hands in front of her as she straightened her spine. "Aunt Dottie said you got enough for a good sketch. Can I see it?"

She'd left the hospital room when he'd resumed his interview with her aunt, needing to take the call from Nick Lawrence. But she hadn't come back until he was finished and had packed up his sketchbook.

After their conversation that morning, he'd understood. Even if her attacker was in jail and not the man who'd attacked her aunt, hearing Mrs. Johnson talk about a man with big hands had brought back some very bad memories.

"Are you sure you want to?" he asked quietly.

She hesitated before shaking her head. "I don't want to, but I need to."

He took out his phone and showed her the photo he'd taken of the image. "I sent it to Lieutenant Lawrence. He'll upload it to the server and it will become evidence in your aunt's assault case."

She visibly steeled herself to look at the photo, staring at the man's face for a long, long moment before her shoulders sagged. "Not him."

Tino covered her folded hands with his. "Good."

She laughed, a brittle sound. "If it had been, at least we'd have an ID for Dottie's attacker."

He wanted to promise that the police would find the man who'd beaten her aunt and left her for dead, but he didn't. He couldn't. Not every case was solved, despite the best efforts of everyone involved.

She swallowed hard. "Thank you for not promising you'd find him. It's a promise with no teeth."

"How did the cops find your attacker?" he asked, unable to help himself. "Don't answer if you don't want to."

"No, it's okay. His mother took him into the ER." Her chin lifted. "I stabbed him in the leg with a screwdriver. He didn't go right away because he didn't want to answer any questions about how he got hurt. The wound got infected. By the time his mother got involved, he was pretty out of it." Her mouth twisted bitterly. "For a while we were in the same hospital. At least he was handcuffed to his bed."

Rage flared up within him and Tino had to take another deep breath. "Good for you," he said, unable to keep the emotion from his voice. He squeezed her hands gently. "I'm glad you had a screwdriver handy. Was it rusty?"

She hiccuped a laugh. "A little, yes. I'd been tightening a screw on the sconce next to my front door, and I'd left the screwdriver on the table in my entryway, intending to put it away later. He was waiting in my kitchen when I got home that night, and he grabbed me when I went to the refrigerator to start making my dinner. He bound my hands and taped my mouth so I couldn't scream. He'd been there long enough to gather up all my knives and any other utensils I could use as a weapon." Her jaw clenched. "He used my own knives on me. Then he freed my hands because he wanted me to . . . well, to . . ."

Tino could guess. "Service him?" He nearly choked on the words, but was glad he'd said them when gratitude filled her eyes. At least she hadn't had to say it.

"I was going to fight him, but I was weak by then. I'd lost a lot of blood. I managed to crawl away, trying to get to the door. He'd 'taken a break' and was drinking my twenty-year port. Guzzling it like it was a beer. Worked in my favor because he was a lot less steady on his feet by that point. I got to the door, but he caught up with me, so I grabbed the screwdriver and stuck it in his leg. He screamed so loud that my neighbor came over to see if I was okay. He ran then, or hobbled, at least. My neighbor called the cops."

Tino didn't know what to say. He could only close his eyes

and be grateful she was still alive, that she'd been clearheaded enough to use the one weapon at her disposal.

She freed one of her hands and patted his. "It's okay, Tino. It's over and done. He's in prison. I'd like to be a better person and say that I hope he's getting the help he needs, but I'm not a better person."

"Neither am I," he ground out. He opened his eyes to find her looking around the restaurant.

"Someone should have come to take our order by now."

She sounded like a restaurant critic, but he had the feeling that falling back into a familiar behavior was how she was coping with reliving her nightmare.

Tino spied Polina standing across the room watching them, her expression concerned. "She's waiting for us to stop talking, trying not to interrupt us."

"Oh." Charlotte forced a smile. "I'm sorry. I didn't mean to criticize. This is a no-criticism date."

Date. Was that what this was? Tino wasn't sure how he felt about that.

You like it.

That he did was supremely stupid. He waved at Polina and she came over to their table.

"Tino," she said warmly, leaning down to hug him. "I've missed you."

"Same. Gino said he came last weekend and he told me all about his amazing meal, even though I was in a hotel room eating burgers from a carryout bag." He said it pitifully, causing both Polina and Charlotte to laugh.

"Poor baby," Charlotte said sarcastically.

"I know," Polina said, then extended her hand. "I'm Polina. This is my place. I hope you enjoy your meal."

"It smells wonderful in here, and I understand your baklava is to die for."

Polina beamed, just as Angela had earlier. Charlotte certainly knew how to compliment restauranteurs.

They placed their orders and Polina left, leaving them in awkward silence.

Once again, Charlotte folded her hands in front of her. "Did you see Mrs. Murphy?"

"I did. She's a real pistol."

Charlotte smiled fondly. "She is. She's been Dottie's neighbor since before I was born. One of my earliest memories is making Christmas cookies with her and Dottie when my parents dropped me off for a weekend visit."

Charlotte's aunt had been a big part of her life, especially since she'd taught at their high school. She'd hung out in Mrs. Johnson's room after class, which was how Tino had gotten to know her better. He'd also hung out in the art room, hungry for the opportunity to paint—and hungry for the praise Mrs. Johnson always heaped upon him.

"I heard about your folks," Tino said. "I'm sorry." Her parents had died in a car accident years ago.

"Thank you. How are your parents?"

Tino shrugged. "They're still married, but they had a falling out over some lies my mother told him awhile back. My mother spends a lot of time with her sister in Jersey these days. I don't miss her, but I feel bad for my father, because I think he does miss her, at least a little bit. He didn't deserve to be manipulated by her. But Dad will be okay. He's got congestive heart disease but still gets around. Still lives on his own, although we all stop by during the week to make sure he's okay. He's constantly surrounded by grandchildren and that makes him happy."

"I'm glad he's doing well. He was always so nice to me."

That his mother hadn't been nice to Charlotte didn't need to be said. Tino's mother had always been critical of her children, which was why he'd spent so much time with the Garganos as a teenager. He'd tried to keep Charlotte out of his mother's way as much as he'd been able.

Charlotte sighed. "I've stalled long enough. Can I see the drawing you made at Mrs. Murphy's house?"

He figured she'd ask. "I only got a sketch of his eyes, because that's all your aunt's neighbor saw. But they're identical to the eyes your aunt described."

Her expression tightened. "So he did come back. Why?"

Tino had a theory, but it would only make her feel more paranoid. More vulnerable. He'd wondered to himself if the man had been looking for Charlotte both times, beating her aunt because Charlotte wasn't there.

It sounded a little crazy, which was why he'd kept it to himself.

"I don't know." Technically not a lie because he didn't know. "But at least we know it wasn't your Memphis stalker."

"Right." She nodded hard. "That will let me sleep better tonight."

"Does your apartment have security?"

"Kind of. The night guard is a little wacky, so we all avoid her. She's one of those end-of-the-world people who has a huge gun safe and tells everyone all about it. I imagine her going home to an underground bunker." She gave an exaggerated shudder. "I wish I'd known before I moved in. I might have picked another apartment building."

"Where do you live?"

"Rittenhouse."

Tino couldn't keep his eyes from popping wide. "Whoa. Restaurant reviews must pay well." That was the swanky part of the city.

"Nah. More like my ex wishes he'd made me sign a prenup. He made money after we got married and I got half of it when we divorced. Which I felt entitled to after he started sleeping with his assistant."

"Then he was a dick, and you're better off without him."

"When we get our drinks, we can toast to that."

"Sounds like a plan. I'm serious, though. Will you be safe there?"

"Yes," she said, but he heard the doubt in her voice.

He had until dinner was over to convince her to stay somewhere else.

With me.

No, not *with me.*

"Maybe you should book a hotel room. Just until the cops find the guy who hurt your aunt."

"If I do that, I might never go home. I'll be fine at home. I have extra locks on my doors, and I'm on the ninth floor. Nobody can get to my window and if they do, the glass isn't breakable. It's the kind that firefighters need a special saw to get through. It's safe."

"Good. You being safe is all I care about." He was not angling to get Charlotte Walsh under his roof.

In his bed.

No, not *in my bed.*

Not tonight anyway. Who knew what the future held?

CHAPTER 4

Charlotte stumbled into her kitchen, grateful for programmable coffee machines. It was her favorite blend, guaranteed to wake her up.

She'd slept badly, tossing and turning, startling at every little sound. She'd come out of the restaurant with Tino the night before and had gotten the same weird feeling that she'd had before going in. Like someone was watching her.

Just my imagination.

Unless it wasn't. It wasn't paranoia when people really wanted to hurt you.

I should have gone to a hotel like Tino said.

But this apartment was her new home. Even though it didn't feel like it. Not yet, anyway. She'd been back in Philly for less than six months. She was still unpacking boxes. But she'd get everything unpacked and put away and then it would be home.

A warm body wound around her legs, and she scooped her

cat into her arms. "You're here," she said to Mrs. Tripplehorn, rubbing her cheek against the cat's soft fur. "So it's home."

She'd fed the cat and poured herself a cup of coffee when she heard voices outside her door. Angry male voices.

And one was familiar.

She checked the peephole and, sure enough, Tino Ciccotelli stood on her doorstep, hands up as if to placate the man shouting at him.

She recognized the man, who lived three doors down. He held a cell phone to his ear, pointing a finger at Tino.

Making sure her robe was firmly tied, she opened the door. "Good morning," she said, raising her voice to be heard. "What seems to be the problem?"

Both men turned to look at her. "He was sleeping on the damn floor!" her neighbor shouted.

She stared at Tino. Sleeping on the floor? Why?

Oh. She'd thought he'd accepted her decision not to go to a hotel way too easily. She'd been right.

More neighbors had started peeking into the hallway and Charlotte needed to shut this confrontation down. *Now.*

"Tino, did you forget your key *again*?" she asked, grabbing him by the sleeve of his jacket and yanking him into her apartment. "I'm so sorry," she said to the neighbor. "It won't happen again."

Because I'm going to read Tino Ciccotelli the riot act.

"This is a respectable building," the man said. "We do not allow homeless people to set up camp."

Charlotte frowned. "He's not homeless." She held out her mug of coffee. "Have you been caffeinated today, sir? Feel free to take my coffee if you need it."

Several neighbors laughed and the man's expression became thunderous. "Watch your step, missy," he snarled. "The condo board can take legal recourse against you."

What an asshole.

Tino opened his mouth to speak, but she yanked him farther into her apartment. "No," she hissed to him, and he wisely closed his mouth. "Sir," she said to her neighbor, "are you threatening me? Please consider your answer carefully. At least one of our neighbors is recording this on her phone. I don't think you want to go viral on the internet. This can be over right now. I apologized. I said it wouldn't happen again. Let it go."

The man scowled. "Trashy bitches," he muttered as he turned on his heel and stomped back to his apartment, scowling at the young woman who was openly recording the entire exchange. "Delete that."

"Oh, I will," the woman said sweetly, rolling her eyes as soon as he'd slammed his apartment door. "Oh, I won't," she called to Charlotte. "I'll hold on to it. If you want me to send the video to you, just let me know." She waved merrily, going back into her apartment.

"We're not all assholes," another woman said. "He's been a grouch from day one. Just ignore him."

Another woman smiled at Tino. "Next time you forget your key, knock on my door, honey. I'll let you in."

The other neighbors groaned good-naturedly and returned to their apartments.

Charlotte closed her door and leaned against it, cradling her mug in her hands, half tempted to toss it at Tino for causing such a fuss.

"Did you sleep on my doormat?"

"I did. It's scratchy."

"I have several. The cat likes to sharpen her claws on them."

Tino's lips twitched. "Is that a threat?" He looked down and his lips curved into a full smile. "Oh, aren't you pretty?"

"Don't try to pick her up," Charlotte said. "She doesn't like strangers."

But he'd already picked the cat up and was giving her head scritches. "Yes, you are a pretty girl. Listen to you purr. Like a motorboat. And your mom says you don't like strangers. Silly Mom. What's your name?"

Of course her cat had fallen prey to Tino's charm. "She's Mrs. Tripplehorn. She had that name when I got her. You want some coffee?"

"Yes. Please yes."

Sighing, she filled a mug for him and started another pot. She allowed herself two cups in the morning, and she wasn't giving up her second cup for anyone. Not even the man who'd slept on her doorstep.

Which should be making her so angry.

But it really wasn't.

It was Tino. *Taking care of me.* Affection warmed her from the inside out.

"How did you get back into the building? I watched you get into the elevator last night."

He gave Mrs. Tripplehorn another stroke before setting her on the floor. "I got to the lobby and the security guard was snoring. I figured you had shit security, so I came back up. Nobody even noticed me until Mr. Congeniality came out this morning and started screaming at me."

"That's not good," she said. "I'll report it. Just . . . don't do that again, okay?"

"I was worried," he said, suddenly more serious than she'd ever seen him. "You thought someone was watching you, before and after dinner. What if you were right? If you're not going to listen to your gut, I will."

She wanted to kiss his cheek but patted it instead, his stubble scratchy against her palm. She wondered how it would feel against her face if she kissed him full on the mouth. Which she really wanted to do, but she pushed the desire down.

That ship's sailed. He's only your friend.

"Thank you," she said. "Just don't do it again, okay?"

"I'm not promising anything."

Because he wasn't the kind of man to lie. It was one of the things she'd loved about him back in the day.

"Well, at least I can make you some breakfast. Have a seat."

"Thank you." He smiled at her, and her heart fluttered in her chest. He was unfairly beautiful, even after having slept on her doorstep all night.

She began gathering ingredients. "French toast and bacon?"

The groan he made was utterly sinful and had her thinking once again about all the things she should not be thinking about.

Which was the other reason she'd tossed and turned. Every time she managed to doze, she'd dreamed of Tino, waking up hot and bothered.

Lonely and needy.

"Yes, please," he said. "Bacon makes everything better."

"It does. What did you tell the neighbor before I opened the door?"

He grinned. "That I forgot my key."

They'd always been in sync. She'd forgotten that. "You're incorrigible."

"You're not the first to say so, and I doubt you'll be the last."

She laughed. "You're such a bad boy." Then she winced. "And I'm bad, too. I haven't called the hospital to check on Dottie yet. My brain cells don't wake up until my second cup of coffee."

"She's fine," Tino said. "I called this morning before the Good Humor Man started yelling at me. She had a good night and her vitals are stronger this morning. Breathing is better. They think the antibiotic is fighting her respiratory infection."

Charlotte exhaled, relieved. "Good. Maybe they'll move her

to a regular room soon." She finished making breakfast and set it in front of Tino with a flourish.

He dove in, inhaling the entire platter of French toast.

His obvious delight made her smile. "I like cooking for people who like my food."

"Then you should love cooking for me, because this is amazing." He cleaned his plate and sat back with a satisfied expression. "You made me French toast once."

She startled, then remembered. "Oh right." She grimaced. "I'd kind of blocked that out."

He chuckled. "I blocked out what happened after your parents came home unexpectedly early from their trip and found us eating French toast in our underwear."

"At least we were wearing that much," she said dryly.

"You were afraid to cook bacon in the nude. Said it would pop and burn you."

It had been the first time he'd stayed over. The night she'd lost her virginity. He'd been so sweet. Bumbling, but sweet. It had been the first time for both of them.

"You always took such good care of me," she murmured.

He sobered. "Then why were you so anxious to leave? Why didn't you want to stay?"

She opened her mouth, but no explanation came forth. And then she was rescued by the ringing of her doorbell.

"Excuse me," she said, placing her napkin on the table and heading for the front door. "I hope it's not that neighbor."

"If it is, we'll call the cops," Tino said, right behind her.

Because of course he'd follow her to the door.

Keeping me safe.

It was hard to be angry with him about that.

A glance through the peephole had her relaxing. "Just a kid I know." She opened the door, smiling at the thirteen-year-old girl who held a large shopping bag. "Kayla, honey, I didn't expect you so early. You want to come in?"

Kayla nodded. "If it's okay. I wanted to bring your bowls back before I went to school." She held out the bag. "I washed them myself, so they're all clean. Thank you so much. My mom says you're the best cook."

Charlotte ran her hand over the girl's hair. "You are so welcome. If you come by tomorrow, I'll have more food made up." She looked over at Tino, who was watching with interest. "Tino, this is Kayla Lewis. Her parents run the corner store. Her dad was shot recently. Her mom has been so busy taking care of the family and the store that she doesn't have time to cook. Kayla, this is my friend Tino."

Kayla looked up at Tino, her smile strained. "Hi."

"Kayla," Tino said warmly. "I'm so sorry about your father."

"He'll be okay," Kayla said, her voice shaky, because it had been a close call. "We're the lucky ones."

"There's been a rash of robberies on the street," Charlotte explained. "A man shot three store owners in one night. Kayla's dad was the only one who made it."

"He's still in the hospital," Kayla said, her eyes filling with tears. "He hasn't woken up yet, but the doctors say that he will. It's an induced coma, so that he can heal."

"Wow, that's a lot for your family to go through," Tino said. "I'm so sorry."

Kayla nodded. "Thank you." She drew a breath and faced Charlotte. "I was wondering if you'd show me how to cook. You can't help us forever, and my mom is so stressed out. She cries all the time and . . ." She blinked, her own tears spilling down her cheeks. "I have to do *something*. I take care of my little brother and sister, but I have to do more."

"I absolutely will," Charlotte promised. "We'll start simple, and I'll show you how to make meals that will be nutritious and yummy. I'll call your mom and set up the times for you to come over. Okay?"

Kayla wiped at her eyes. "Thank you. You've been so nice to us. To the other families, too." She looked at Tino. "Charlotte cooks for all of us, all three of our families. One lost their grandma. She ran the dry cleaners. The other lost their grandpa. He owned the pizza place. He was closing up when the man came in with a gun. It's been bad."

Tino slowly blew out a breath. "I read about the violence. I didn't realize it was this neighborhood. I'm glad Charlotte is helping you."

Kayla's smile was wobbly. "Me too. I have to go to school now. Can I come over tonight?"

"Of course. I'll clear it with your mom."

Kayla threw her arms around Charlotte, her tears becoming sobs. Charlotte hugged her back, letting the girl hold on as long as she needed to, stroking her hair and saying nothing at all.

Words didn't really help. She'd learned that after the car accident all those years ago and again after the attack. Actions were important.

Actions like sleeping on a person's doorstep to keep them safe.

She gave Tino a helpless look. He returned it, fetching a box of tissues from the coffee table. He pushed a handful of tissues into Kayla's hand, and the girl wiped at her face before stepping away.

"I'm sorry," Kayla said, embarrassed.

"You hush right now," Charlotte said. "You're fine, and any time you want to cry, you come on up. Okay?"

"Okay," Kayla sniffled. "I'll see you later. Nice to meet you, Tino."

"Same," Tino said and walked her to the door. "Are you going to be safe going to school?"

"Yes. My cousin is waiting for me in the lobby. He drove my mom to the store this morning and he'll take me to school. I have to go or I'll make him late."

Tino closed the door, his expression hard to read.

"Tino?" Charlotte prompted.

"Were you a customer of all the places that the gunman hit?"

"Yes. Why?"

"Because I don't like coincidences. How do you pay when you go to these places?"

"Cash." Because a credit card left a paper trail, and she was terrified to let that happen again. "Why?"

"Did any of the places have your address?"

"Both the pizza and the dry-cleaning place do because they deliver. Tino, you're scaring me."

There was an intensity to his gaze that had her shivering, and not in a good way.

"You're a common denominator, Charlotte. I don't like that. I'm going to let Nick Lawrence know. It might be nothing, but I want someone checking into it."

"Okay." Charlotte's stomach was clenching and she needed to be alone for a few minutes. "I'm going to get dressed."

Tino nodded as he made his call. "Nick, it's Tino."

She closed the door to her bedroom, muting his voice, and sat on the edge of her bed. It couldn't be connected. That was simply ridiculous.

She looked up at the knock on the door, startled. She hadn't gotten dressed. She hadn't even moved from where she sat on the bed and ten minutes had passed.

"Tino?"

"Yeah, can I come in?"

He sounded . . . upset. She wanted to tell him no, to go away, that she didn't want any more bad news. But that would be foolish, and Charlotte prided herself on not being foolish.

"Yes."

He entered, stopping a foot inside the door. "I remember that quilt."

She ran her hand over the old fabric. "My grandmother made it for me."

"It was on your bed when you lived at home."

"One of the only things I took with me. Tino, what did Lieutenant Lawrence say?"

"First, he hadn't put together that the murders happened on your street. The case is being handled by my brother Vito's department. Nick's going to see if your aunt's case connects."

"Okay. What's the second thing?"

"He got a call from the prison in Memphis this morning. The man who attacked you is dead. He was stabbed in the prison exercise yard two weeks ago. No one is sure who did it. It's still under investigation."

Charlotte's mouth fell open. "Why didn't they tell me?"

"I don't know why someone in Memphis didn't call. Nick was going to call you after eight to tell you. He didn't want to wake you up."

"What am I supposed to do next?"

"We're going to see Vito. I called him after I was done talking to Nick. My sister-in-law is pregnant, and yesterday her doctor put her on bed rest. Vito took today off, so we're going to his house. I want his opinion on all this."

Charlotte nodded numbly. "Okay."

* * *

PHILADELPHIA, PENNSYLVANIA
WEDNESDAY, MARCH 30, 8:15 A.M.

TINO BROUGHT his car to a stop in front of Vito's house, then turned to face Charlotte, who'd been silent throughout the entire drive.

"Vito . . ." Tino sighed. "He was the one I talked to when you left. He was the one who got my life moving forward again."

Charlotte still stared straight ahead. "He's still angry with me."

"A little." He winced. "Maybe a lot. But he's a good guy. A great cop. He'll do his job. He'll find out who killed the two shop owners on your street, put a third in critical condition, and potentially beat your aunt and left her for dead."

"*If* they're connected."

"If," Tino allowed. But it was possible. They at least had to check it out.

"Then let's get this over with so your sister-in-law can rest."

"That's going to be a challenge. Her resting, I mean. Sophie's like the Energizer Bunny, always doing something. She makes me tired just watching her." He got out of the car and went around to open her door, his heartbeat accelerating when she took the hand he offered.

It's what friends do, he reminded himself. *Friends.*

She squared her shoulders and started walking. "Time to face the music."

"Charlotte." He tugged on her hand until she looked up at him. "You're not on trial here. If he brings up the past, I'll shut him down. You're here to offer him information about the shop owners who were targeted. He'll want to know your routine, any messages you've received, anything that might help him connect these cases, if there is a connection. But you're not here to answer for the choices you made twenty-four years ago. Okay?"

Her smile was wobbly. "I believe you. Not sure about Vito's reception, though. He let me know in no uncertain terms what he thought of me back then. If he's still harboring even a fraction of his anger, it's still going to be uncomfortable."

Tino frowned. "He talked to you then?"

"Yes. Came to my house." She looked away. "Yelled a lot. Wanted to know if I'd been cheating on you. If I had someone else waiting. I didn't. I don't think he believed me, but that's the truth, Tino."

"I believe you, and for now, that's all that matters." He led her to the house that had belonged to Sophie's grandmother. She'd left it to Sophie when she died, and Sophie and Vito had made it a real home.

Tino wasn't jealous.

Okay, maybe a little jealous. But it wasn't like he didn't want Vito to have this. He just wanted the same for himself.

He loved his brother. He really did. But if Vito hurt Charlotte's feelings today, or made her feel even a little bad, Tino was going to have words with him.

And that Vito had gone to Charlotte's house back then? That he'd accused her? Tino couldn't think about that right now. He might say something to Vito that he couldn't take back. He'd process later, then figure out what, if anything, he needed to address.

It *had* been twenty-four years. If Vito backed off his attitude toward Charlotte, Tino could let Vito's interference go, too.

He'd lifted his fist to knock when Vito opened the door, his brother's eyes shadowed and worried.

Because Sophie was on bed rest. Tino wanted to kick himself for forgetting about that for even a moment.

"How's Sophie?" he asked.

"She's fine!" Sophie called from the living room. "Come in."

Vito held the door open wider so they could enter. "What

she said." He closed the door, letting his gaze drop to the hand Tino pressed at the small of Charlotte's back before meeting her gaze squarely. "Welcome to our home, Charlotte."

Charlotte blinked, startled. "Um . . . thank you."

Tino lifted his brows in question, and Vito shrugged. "Sophie threatened to kick my ass if I didn't let old grudges go. So they're gone. Come into the living room and make yourself comfortable. Can I get you anything to eat or drink?"

Tino wanted to laugh. Sophie must have really gotten serious about kicking Vito's ass. He was being super polite.

"I'm fine, thank you." Charlotte followed Vito into the living room where Sophie lay on the sofa, a pile of pillows at her back.

She looked pale, with dark circles under her eyes. Tino felt a shaft of fear pierce his heart. "Soph."

Sophie rolled her eyes. "I'm fine. Blood pressure's a little high."

Vito huffed. "Preeclampsia. Mild, which is the only reason she's here and not in the hospital."

"I'm at thirty-six weeks. If they can get me to thirty-seven or thirty-eight, all will be well. I'm being a good girl." She looked around Tino to Charlotte, who'd hung back. "Please come closer, Charlotte. I've wanted to meet you since Tino said you'd come back to Philly."

Tino remembered his manners. "Charlotte, this is my sister-in-law, Sophie. Sophie, this is Charlotte Walsh."

Charlotte approached, her trepidation clear. "I'm so sorry to be disturbing you."

Sophie smiled. "You're not. Sit, please. All of you. I'm getting a crick in my neck looking up at you."

Tino gestured to a loveseat and Charlotte joined him there. "What do you know about the crimes on Charlotte's street, Vito?" he asked, getting down to business. This wasn't a social call. Not with Charlotte so tense and Sophie needing her rest.

"Not much," Vito admitted. "The killer of the shop owners used a gun with a silencer, and Mrs. Johnson's attacker didn't. We never considered that the cases could be connected. I'm still far from convinced that they are, but we need to at least explore the possibility."

"Especially since we have a sketch of Mrs. J's attacker," Tino said. "I sent it to Nick last night."

Vito nodded. "He sent it to me while you were driving over. Mrs. Johnson's sketch and the one you did based on the neighbor's eyewitness account. You didn't recognize him, Charlotte?"

Charlotte shook her head. "I didn't. I mean . . . To be honest, I was just concerned with whether or not he was the same man who attacked me. I can look again."

"Not right now," Vito said. "Tell me about your relationships with the victims on your street."

"Well, there's Mr. Lewis who runs the convenience store. He's the one who's in critical condition." She grimaced. "But you know that already. Sorry."

"Charlotte," Sophie said quietly. "Breathe. We're here to help you and nothing more. If you need to ramble, my husband will deal. He's used to it, because I ramble when I'm stressed, too."

Charlotte sucked in a desperate breath and let it out. "Okay. Mr. Lewis isn't usually on night duty at the store, but he was that night. His regular night clerk was sick. He's a nice man, and I hate that this happened to him and his family. They're just trying to make a living. And if this is connected to me . . ."

"If it is, it's still not your fault," Vito said firmly. "It's the fault of whoever shot him. Did you know him well?"

"Not that well, no. We were acquaintances, mainly. I know his wife better. But I know he likes hockey and football and that he's so proud of his children. He works hard to give them a good life. He talks about them to whoever will listen."

"And you listened?" Vito asked.

"I did. I was new in the neighborhood and he made me feel welcome. Told me where to get the best pizza and where to get my dry cleaning done." She stopped abruptly. "They pushed each other's businesses. The three of them kept business cards and posted flyers for the others' stores."

"Just those three?" Sophie asked. "Or did they push the other businesses on the street, too?"

"Just those three. They were friends. Mr. Lewis in the corner store, Mr. Lombardi who owned the pizza place, and Mrs. Fadil who owned the dry cleaner's. If I asked about a certain service, like fresh flowers, they'd name a few places, but there was no feeling behind it, no real recommendation."

"Interesting," Vito murmured. "Nobody's brought that up yet."

"I'm new to the neighborhood," Charlotte said. "Maybe the people you talked to had been there long enough that they didn't remember."

"Possibly. Go back to what you know about the victims, please."

"Mr. Lombardi's sons worked for him, all but the youngest. Mr. Lombardi said he was okay with it, that his son was following his dreams, but he was worried about him. The son's a schoolteacher in one of the more ... troubled schools."

"He was afraid his son would be hurt," Sophie said.

Charlotte nodded sadly. "Mr. Lombardi was terrified there would be a school shooting. But then he himself got shot." She dabbed at her wet eyes with a tissue. "Sorry. I really liked him. He was jolly, with a big laugh, and he always had a smile for me. The neighborhood won't be the same without him."

"And Mrs. Fadil?" Vito asked.

"She was an American citizen. She was so proud of that. Had a flag on the wall and everything. The first time I took my clothes to her store, she told me that she'd gotten her citizenship fifteen years ago. Told me about building the business with her husband, who died a few years ago. Cancer. She told me about her children and her grandchildren, who all live in or around Philly. She told me about her parents, who still live in Morocco. We talked a lot about cooking. When I told her I knew how to cook with a tagine and owned three of them, she came around the counter and hugged me. Then she gave me her mother's recipe for kefta. I made it that evening and . . ." Her voice broke. "I took her some."

"You knew them all quite well," Vito said, sounding surprised.

"I just listened. All three of them were friendly and I . . . I just listened."

"No 'just' about it," Sophie said. "Not everyone listens."

Charlotte wiped her eyes. "I guess I was lonely. I came back home, but it wasn't the same. Nothing was really the same. I think they knew — the three storeowners — that I needed the connection."

"When did you come back? And why?" Vito asked, but there was no accusation in his tone.

Tino would have put a stop to it if there had been.

"I came back about six months ago. I got out of the hospital in Memphis and I couldn't sleep in my bed. Literally." She glanced at Tino. "The man who attacked me had destroyed the mattress and punched holes in the wall."

"Sonofabitch," Tino muttered. "I'm sorry."

Her smile was small but genuine. "Thank you. Me too." She sighed and turned back to Vito. "I felt terrified to enter my own home, Lieutenant."

Vito flinched. "You don't have to call me lieutenant. I'm just Vito. Please."

She dropped her gaze to the tissue she held in her fisted hand. "Okay. Anyway, I couldn't go home. I rented a furnished apartment where I could recuperate and figure out my next steps. I realized how alone I was. My ex-husband got our friends in the divorce, and my real name was now associated with my pen name because of the news reports on my attack. There were reporters on my doorstep and letters in my mailbox from angry restaurant owners I'd given bad reviews to in the past. Then there were the emails." She grimaced. "A lot of people thought I deserved what I'd gotten. Even my ex's family. It was isolating. I couldn't breathe. And Aunt Dottie is getting up in years. I decided to come back to Philly and take care of her."

"And did you?" Vito asked. "Take care of her, I mean."

Charlotte frowned. "Of course I did. I know you don't like me, but I'm not a bad person." She threw a pained glance at Tino. "Not anymore, anyway."

Vito shook his head, speaking before Tino could say a word. "You misunderstand my question. I meant, were you a constant presence at her house? Was it just taking her out to dinner once a week, or were you there every day?"

"Oh." Charlotte exhaled, looking both sheepish and relieved. "Not every day, but if I wasn't in New York or Baltimore doing restaurant reviews, I was at her house. I didn't realize how lonely she'd become, too. She hid it from me whenever I called her. My uncle is gone and a lot of her oldest friends are, too. So I was there at least four or five times a week. Sometimes we'd go out, sometimes I'd bring a p—" She stopped abruptly, her eyes going wide with horrified realization. "Pizza. I'd bring her pizza from Lombardi's. If someone was watching me . . ." She covered her mouth with her hand. "They started killing that night at Lombardi's. The man started there, then went to Mrs. Fadil's dry cleaner's and then to Mr. Lewis's convenience store."

Tino hadn't known the order of the murders, but Charlotte was right. That the owner of the pizza place was first was too much coincidence.

But then Charlotte shook her head. "God. I sound crazy. I've been paranoid since my attack. This is not connected to me. It can't be."

"I'd completely agree with you," Vito said, "but it appears that your aunt's attacker came back to her house. That she's in the hospital has been on the news. Her attacker knew she wasn't there. We can't ignore the possibility that he could have been looking for you."

Charlotte swallowed hard. "But why?" she asked, her wounded tone hurting Tino's heart. "I didn't do anything to anyone. I mind my own business."

"Except when you're criticizing people's restaurants," Vito said, then held up a hand when Tino opened his mouth to protest the words. "I'm not saying she deserves it, Tino. She most certainly does not deserve it. I'm only saying that her profession has the potential of making her a target."

It was fair, Tino thought, but he frowned as he nodded.

Vito turned back to Charlotte. "Tino said that your Memphis attacker got your address from the newspaper's office using your tax information and that you're still reviewing under your old alias. If your real name and your alias were linked in Memphis, how do you know someone hasn't tracked you here?"

"I don't, I suppose," she murmured. "But I've been really careful not to leave a trail for another stalker to follow, either electronic or paper. I'm not writing for a paper anymore, so I'm not on anyone's payroll. I started a blog and used some of the notoriety I got after the attack as free advertising, to be honest. I gave a few interviews to reporters I trusted. I let people know I was still reviewing, but I'd be a traveling reviewer. I've done reviews in restaurants in Atlanta and St. Louis along with the New York and Baltimore restaurants."

"But if someone still wanted to find you, they could," Vito said gently. "Do you have an apartment here in the city? There

will be rental records or property records. Mortgage information. Lots of ways someone could find you if they really
wanted to."

She shook her head. "I bought my condo with cash and in
the name of a corporation I formed so that my name wouldn't be
in the property records. I've made it as difficult as I can for
someone to find me."

Vito's brows lifted. "Cash? In Rittenhouse?"

She lifted her chin. "I got the house and half my ex-
husband's assets in the divorce. Then I sold my house in
Memphis, plus I got a settlement from the newspaper in
exchange for not suing them for giving out my personal information. I used it to buy the condo. I figured I was paying for
security, and that's more important to me than it used to be."

"Completely understandable," Sophie said kindly. "I'd do
the same thing."

Vito nodded, his expression the one that said he was thinking. "Okay, so . . . let's assume for a moment that the murders on
your street *are* connected to the assault on your aunt. And that
someone saw you bringing pizza from Lombardi's, which was
why they started their murdering rampage at the pizza shop."
He closed his eyes, quiet for a few moments. Then he opened
his eyes on a sigh. "Their files were stolen. Lombardi's and
Fadil's, which makes sense. They do deliveries. They kept
addresses of their regulars on file."

"So a killer might have Charlotte's address," Tino said flatly.

"Then why go to her aunt's house at all?" Sophie asked. "If
he had Charlotte's address, why didn't he go to her
apartment?"

"She has security." Tino made a face. "Kind of. Not great
security at night, but maybe he saw the person at the desk and
decided not to chance it."

Sophie looked skeptical. "Well, why not just wait for her

outside her building? And why didn't he demand to know where Charlotte was when he assaulted her aunt?"

"Good points," Vito allowed. He picked up his tablet from the coffee table and swiped through several pages. "This is the report on your aunt's assault. She doesn't mention that he said anything, but she did say that he searched every room, dragging her along behind him. He even checked the closets and under the beds. When he didn't find what he was looking for, he began to beat her." He looked up, his expression softening when he saw that Charlotte had paled. "I'm sorry, Charlotte. I know this is difficult."

"He took her phone," Charlotte said thickly. "He beat her until she told him the password, then beat her some more when he'd searched her phone. But she didn't have my new address in her contacts. And he wouldn't have gotten it from either Mr. Lombardi or Mrs. Fadil."

Tino covered her trembling hand with his. "Why?" he asked gently. "Why didn't your aunt have your address in her phone?"

Vito put his tablet down, giving her his undivided attention.

She clutched Tino's hand like a lifeline. "I told Dottie that I'd had some trouble with my ex. That I didn't want anyone knowing where I lived. To my knowledge, she doesn't know about last year's attack. I never told her and she doesn't go online for news. She knew the divorce had been ugly, so she never asked me any questions, just did what I asked. I've brought her to my place a few times. Made supper for her. But ninety-five percent of the time I go to her house because it's hard for her to get in and out of a car."

"And Mr. Lombardi and Mrs. Fadil?" Tino asked. "Why didn't they have your address if they delivered to you?"

"They did, but not under my name. I told them the same thing, that I'd had trouble with my ex and didn't want to be tracked. Whenever I'd place an order, they'd use 'Jane Smith' and I'd pay with cash. They were so kind to me. They can't have been killed because of me." Her voice cracked. "They can't."

"This is not your fault," Tino whispered fiercely.

"He's right," Vito said. "Not your fault at all. So, once again, if we assume that these cases are connected and that he made the connection to Lombardi's because you brought pizza to your aunt, that means that he was watching your aunt's house. How did he make the connection between you and your aunt?"

"I don't know," Charlotte said helplessly. "We don't have the same last name, and I didn't tell anyone where I was moving when I left Memphis."

"Your moving company would have known," Sophie said.

"No, because I moved myself. I only brought a few things with me. Just boxes of documents and records. A few photos. I drove from Memphis to Philly by way of Atlanta. I took the long way, reviewing restaurants along the way."

"And the man who attacked you in Memphis?" Sophie asked. "Are you sure he's still in prison?"

"He's dead," Vito said.

Sophie frowned. "You didn't tell me that."

Vito frowned back. "You're supposed to be resting."

"He was killed in the exercise yard in the prison two weeks ago," Tino said. "Nick Lawrence is waiting for more information. The prison is investigating."

"So this is someone new. Seems like the options are—" Sophie held up her fingers as she counted. "One—another restaurant owner got angry and managed to find out where you moved to, but that still leaves the question of how they connected your aunt to you. Two—could your ex be retaliating for any reason? Or three—this new guy is completely random and unrelated to your job or past."

Charlotte shook her head. "It's not my ex. He just wanted me out of his life, and we didn't have contact after the divorce, not until I was in the hospital. He came to see me, brought me flowers, then told me that he'd told me so, that my reviews would end up getting me in trouble. That I should have listened to him."

"What a dick," Sophie muttered.

Charlotte laughed, a slightly hysterical sound. "He is. I don't think another restaurant owner would be mad at me, at least not based on my recent reviews. I've made sure they were all positive. If a review was too scathing, I set the review aside in a special folder. I'm . . ." She sighed. "I'm too afraid to publish anything negative right now. Maybe forever. Which means I probably won't be successful when people get tired of A-plus reviews."

"I'm sorry," Sophie said softly. "I hate that some asshole has made you afraid."

Charlotte managed a small smile. "Thank you." She turned to Vito. "So what's next?"

"We canvass your street again, take another look at security cameras. Dig deeper. Someone had to have seen something. As for you, be careful. If someone wants to follow you, they might guess that you'll be at the hospital. They could wait for you there."

Tino's gut churned. That someone could even have followed Charlotte last night . . . He was so glad he'd slept on her doorstep. He stood and went to give Sophie a kiss on the cheek. "You keep being a good girl. My new nephew needs to cook a little more."

Sophie smiled at him. "I will." She glanced at Charlotte, then whispered. "Keep her safe?"

"I will," he whispered back.

He waited until he and Charlotte were back in his car before turning to her. "I don't want you to stay in your apartment. Not alone."

She looked out the window. "Are you offering to stay with me?"

"No, I'm asking you to come and stay with me."

She shook her head. "You're all the way out in Mount Airy. I need to be closer to the hospital in case Dottie needs me." She bit at her lip. "I don't want to be stupid, Tino. I'll get a hotel room close to the hospital. I'll get one with good security. You don't have to feel responsible for me."

"I don't feel responsible for you." Which was a total lie. "Dammit, Charlotte, you need to lie low for a while. Let me help you. Pick a hotel, and I'll take you to your place to pack a bag. I can get a cot brought in or something. But I don't want you to be alone."

She was quiet for a long moment, then surprised him by nodding. "All right. Thank you. I don't want me to be alone, either."

He reached over and gripped her chin lightly, tugging until she faced him. She was crying again, and it made his own eyes sting. "Friends don't let friends be alone."

CHAPTER 5

"THIS ISN'T what I meant by lying low," Tino grumbled, sitting on a stool at Charlotte's kitchen island as she organized ingredients.

Charlotte knew he was irritated by her refusal to give up her evening plan of cooking for her neighbors. She hadn't remembered about Kayla, though. Not until Mrs. Lewis texted, asking if it was really okay if Kayla came over for a cooking lesson.

Charlotte and Tino had been at the hospital, sitting at Dottie's side. Charlotte had responded with *Of course!* to Mrs. Lewis's text, not letting Tino know until they'd left the ICU because she'd known he'd argue. She did not want Dottie worried that her niece might not be safe.

"Look, I did what you suggested," she said, keeping her hands busy and her back to his disapproving face. "I got a hotel for tonight—a suite with two separate bedrooms so you don't have to sleep outside the door again. But I made a promise, Tino. A promise to a scared thirteen-year-old girl. She's coming over any minute. We will cook, and then you and I will see Kayla home, and then we'll deliver the food to the other families. The Lombardis and the Fadils both live near Aunt Dottie's house, and the Lewises are in Point Breeze. And then we'll go to the hotel."

That the families who owned the shops in Rittenhouse Square didn't live there was no surprise. Rittenhouse was a pricey neighborhood, but the areas where the families lived weren't bad. Charlotte hadn't been nervous about going there before, but she hadn't known a psycho might be following her then.

And it wasn't like she was going alone. Tino had already said he wasn't leaving her side.

"And if your aunt's attacker is waiting outside your apartment for you to leave?" Tino demanded. "He'll just follow you."

"He may have done that already," Charlotte said, trying not to sound as frightened as she felt. The whole situation was surreal. Abruptly, she stopped reorganizing the ingredients she'd already organized twice and bowed her head. "I'm scared, okay? I don't want to believe this has anything to do with me—either the murders or Dottie's assault. But if it does? I'm scared. And when I'm scared, I cook."

She heard the stool on which he sat scrape over the floor, and then strong hands were on her shoulders, warm and steady. "I'm just trying to keep you safe."

She leaned back into his touch. "I know."

"But I didn't fully consider how this was affecting you, and for that I'm sorry. I'll back off, but I'm going to call in some reinforcements. Gino was a bouncer part-time for a while. He's a big guy, intimidating. I'm going to ask him to follow us tonight when we leave here. Just to be safe."

"Thank you." She laughed shakily. "I never meant to be so much trouble, but it seems to follow me."

"None of this is your fault. Even if there is a connection, it's not your fault."

"I guess that depends on why this hypothetical stalker is after me. Maybe I made him angry. Maybe I gave his restaurant a bad review. Maybe I cut him off in traffic."

He gave her a gentle shake. "Still not your fault. Normal people don't use violence in those situations." He ran his hands down her arms, making her shiver. Then he stepped around her to study the ingredients she'd laid out. "What's for dinner?"

"I'm making roast chicken and a beef stir-fry. I've got enough to make meals for all three families and also some for your brother and sister-in-law. Sophie's not going to be able to cook, and Vito's not going to have time. Someone has to feed their kids."

Tino turned to her, his eyes warm and full of gratitude. "Thank you."

She opened her mouth to tell him it was no trouble, but as their gazes held, the gratitude in his eyes shifted to . . . heat. Desire.

She drew in an unsteady breath, leaning toward him before she realized she was doing so. He cupped her cheek and it felt so good. Then he leaned closer, his mouth an inch from hers.

"Charlotte," he murmured.

Her heart fluttered in her chest. If only he'd call her Charlie again, it would be perfect. "Can you—"

The moment was broken by the ringing of the doorbell. She lurched back, his hand falling from her cheek to his side.

He inhaled sharply, looking away. "It's probably the girl. Kayla. Go answer it."

She started for the door, glancing over her shoulder to find him on her heels. He wasn't going to let her answer the door alone.

It made her feel better.

She checked the peephole to make sure it was Kayla, opening the door when she was sure that it was. "Kayla, come in."

Kayla entered a little warily, looking from Charlotte to Tino. "Are you okay?" she asked Charlotte.

Charlotte wrapped her arm around Kayla's shoulders. "I am fine. Let's get started, because this is a school night and you have an early day tomorrow." She handed Kayla an apron when they got to the kitchen. "You can keep this one and use it at home when you make this yourself."

They set to work, Kayla a quick learner. The girl was so good at slicing vegetables for the stir-fry that Charlotte knew she'd had some experience cooking.

"I cut up vegetables for my dad when he cooks," Kayla said when Charlotte mentioned her skill. "I never really paid attention to the cooking part, though. I was always ready to be done, to go do things with my friends." She paused, her expression miserable. "I should have spent more time with my dad. What if he dies? I should have stayed with him when he made dinner and not run out to hang out with my friends."

Charlotte dried her hands and smoothed a hand over Kayla's hair. "Honey, I don't know your dad very well, but he is so proud of you. Everyone who walked in his store knew that. He told me that he wished that he didn't have to depend on you kids so much for help stocking shelves, that he wanted you to have normal childhoods. I'm sure he didn't mind that you went to hang with your friends as long as you did your chores."

"I did. I always did."

She lifted Kayla's chin with her finger. "Then don't be sad about wanting to spend time with your friends. Now, are you ready to season the chicken?"

Kayla forced a grin, but the shadows in her eyes remained. "Do I have to stick my hand up inside it?"

Charlotte chuckled. "No."

"Then I'm ready."

"Good. The chicken is the easy meal. We just drizzle some olive oil on it, then rub this seasoning mix into it, and then put it in the oven with some veggies. I'm sending home a bag of the seasoning mix with you, and I'll email you the recipe, along with written instructions for everything we'll do tonight."

"And the beef and broccoli? Is that easy, too?" Kayla asked.

"It is. I normally use a wok for that, but I'm going to start you with a skillet. Maybe next time we can play with the wok."

Kayla's smile bloomed, sweet and genuine. "Next time?"

"Do you want more lessons?"

"Yes, ma'am. I do."

"Then that's what we'll do."

They worked together well, Kayla soaking up the attention. Tino stayed quiet behind them, only leaving his seat at the island to grab vegetables to snack on. Most of the time he was bent over his sketch pad, his pencil flying, and Charlotte remembered the boy he'd been, always drawing something.

Usually me.

"I kept them for a long time," she murmured while Kayla was occupied with adding oil to a skillet for the stir-fry. "The sketches you made of me."

Tino looked up, his eyes meeting hers, dark and intense. "You did?"

"Until my ex found one. He was angry. Said it was like I was cheating on him. In a way, he was right. He was . . . well, he wasn't you."

Tino sucked in a harsh breath. "You wanted him to be me?"

Her smile was sad. "By then I'd realized what I'd given up."

"Then why didn't you come home?" he whispered.

To me went unspoken.

"I was embarrassed," she whispered back. "And afraid. I

figured I'd burned the bridge with you and you'd never forgive me."

"I did. Eventually," he added wryly. "Took a while." His gaze flicked behind her, and she turned to find Kayla quietly waiting.

"I finished adding the oil," Kayla said. "But I didn't want to interrupt."

Charlotte knew she was blushing. "You're not interrupting. We were just . . . talking."

Kayla's lifted eyebrows spoke volumes about what she thought of Charlotte's lame attempt at denial.

"Fine," Charlotte said. "We were reminiscing. We dated in high school."

Kayla's expression morphed, going all heart-eyed. "That's so cute!"

Tino chuckled. "Here. Give this to your mom." He tore off a sheet from his sketch pad and held it for her to see. He'd drawn Charlotte and Kayla prepping the vegetables, both wearing expressions of concentration. "This way you can include her in the experience, even if she's not here with you."

Kayla looked stunned. "You're so good. That looks just like us."

"He's a sketch artist," Charlotte said, hearing the pride in her voice and not caring if she sounded like a sappy fool. "He works for the police. He sketched the man who hurt my aunt."

Kayla turned to Charlotte. "You didn't say that your aunt was hurt."

Charlotte hesitated, because she hadn't intended to say it now, but it had slipped out. "You've already got enough on your mind with your dad. No reason to add to it with my issues."

Kayla frowned. "But you're dealing with my issues and yours. I can do the same for you, Charlotte."

Tino cleared his throat. "She's right."

Charlotte threw an irritated glance at Tino before returning her focus to Kayla. "You're right. My aunt was beaten in her home."

She wasn't sure if she should add that the police thought that Kayla's father's assailant might be the same man who attacked Dottie, but Tino took the decision out of her hands.

"My brother is a Homicide lieutenant," he said. "He's exploring a possible connection between Charlotte's aunt's assault and the shootings on this street."

Kayla stared at Charlotte. "Why didn't you tell me?"

"What purpose would it serve?" Charlotte asked. "You're worried enough about your father. You're trying to keep your family fed. Trying to help your mom. There isn't anything you can add to the investigation. I'm sure you told the police everything you knew, which couldn't have been much because you weren't there that night your dad was shot."

She expected Kayla to nod briskly and get back to the food, but the girl stood in the middle of her kitchen looking like a deer caught in the headlights.

"Kayla?" Tino asked softly. "You weren't there that night, were you?"

Kayla swallowed and turned for the skillet. "What do I add next?"

Charlotte took the skillet off the burner and set it aside. "Kayla. Were you there?"

Kayla hung her head, like she was too tired to hold it up any longer. And then she nodded.

Charlotte carefully turned the girl to face them. "Why were you in your dad's store in the middle of the night, honey?"

Kayla's eyes had filled with tears. "I was out with my friends."

At two a.m.? Charlotte wanted to demand, but that wouldn't help Kayla. "And?"

"We got hungry. I didn't know Dad was there. He wasn't supposed to be."

"His regular night clerk was sick," Charlotte said.

Kayla blinked, sending tears down her cheeks. "Jason is the night clerk. He's twenty-one, and some of my friends think he's hot. He always lets us get snacks and never tells my dad. So when we're out, we always stop at the store. But it wasn't Jason. It was Dad at the counter. He was so mad at me. My friends ran. Left me there. He was yelling at me, saying this was why I was failing math, because I was out so late." A little sob bubbled up. "I didn't go out on school nights. Just Saturdays. Mom and Dad were always sleeping by then, so it was easy to sneak out."

"And then the man came in with the gun?" Tino asked softly.

Kayla nodded miserably. "I'd backed away from the counter when he came in. I was in the snack aisle, trying to get away from my dad, because he was yelling at me. The man had the gun in his hand when he ran in, and my dad had us trained on what to do if that happened. I ran out the back door and called 911."

Charlotte frowned at Tino. "Wouldn't your brother have the 911 transcripts? Wouldn't he have known Kayla was a witness? That she called it in?"

Kayla looked away. "It's a burner. All my friends have them. Our parents monitor our phones, so we get burners. I just gave 911 the address. I didn't give them my name. I panicked and hung up."

"Oh," Charlotte murmured. "What happened after you called 911?"

"I ran through the alley to the front of the store. I figured the guy would clean out the register, and then he'd run. Dad would be shaken up and I wanted to help him. But then police and ambulances came and blocked the road, and I couldn't get closer."

"Mr. Lombardi at the pizza place managed to call 911 before the man shot him," Tino said. "I read that online. He was the first person shot. The police were already on their way to the neighborhood when you called, Kayla."

She nodded, her shoulders shaking with sobs. "I know."

Charlotte stroked Kayla's hair, then cupped her face in both hands. "Then what, honey? What did you do when the police came?"

"I got scared. I ran." Kayla pressed her face to Charlotte's shoulder. "I ran like a coward while my dad was bleeding."

"The medics had arrived," Charlotte said, trying for logical pragmatism. "They were able to help him. There really wasn't anything you could have done."

Kayla yanked her head back to glare up at Charlotte. "I could have held his hand so he wasn't alone!"

Charlotte bit her lip. "I'm sorry. You're right." Because that was exactly how she'd felt about Dottie. "I understand. I wanted to be with my aunt, to hold her hand. To let her know she wasn't alone." She wiped Kayla's cheeks with her thumbs. "But I think your dad would have been happier to know you went home where you'd be safe."

"I was a coward."

"You were human," Charlotte countered, looking at Tino for help.

Tino came around the island and bent so he was looking Kayla in the eye. "You feel guilty that you weren't with him to hold his hand. And maybe because you haven't told the cops that you were there?"

Kayla exhaled heavily. "Yeah. The cops never asked me if I saw anything, so I didn't say anything."

"Because they thought you'd been home at the time," Tino said. "But you saw his face," he added in a careful tone.

She shook her head. "Only for a second, when he first came in. He wore a hoodie and it hid his face the rest of the time."

But a glimpse just might be enough, Charlotte thought.

"Can you describe him for me?" Tino asked, keeping his voice calm.

Kayla closed her eyes. "I don't want him to know that I saw him. He kept screaming, 'Where is she? Where is she?' when I was running to the back door. He knew I was there. If he finds out I told..."

Tino's jaw tightened. "Did he see you?"

"I didn't think so, but he must have. He was yelling like he had."

Tino straightened and met Charlotte's gaze. "He was looking for a 'she.'"

For me, Charlotte thought, panic closing her throat. She could only nod, but inside, she was screaming. *No, no, no. It cannot be me. I can't be the connection.*

Because two people were dead and two others were in critical condition.

How could she survive being the reason for that?

Tino returned his attention to Kayla. "If you can tell me what you saw, I can draw it. You can tell me if it's close."

"There were cameras," Kayla protested. "They'll be better than drawings."

"None of the cameras caught him full in the face." Tino hesitated. "Kayla, knowing if this man is the same one who hurt Charlotte's aunt might help the cops catch him. You can help your father that way. Will you tell me what you saw?"

Kayla straightened her shoulders. "Yes."

* * *

"IS SHE OKAY?" Gino asked as Tino closed the bedroom door behind him.

Tino had been checking on Charlotte frequently, worried at the way she'd turned in on herself when he'd finished the sketch of the man Kayla had seen the night of the shootings.

"Not really," Tino murmured, pouring himself a cup of coffee. "She fully cooperated with Vito when he asked her questions, but down deep she'd convinced herself that she wasn't the common denominator. She wanted to believe that the man who'd attacked her aunt was different than the man who'd shot three shop owners on her street."

"But it's the same guy," Gino said, retrieving the hazelnut creamer that Tino preferred.

With a weary smile of thanks, Tino doctored his coffee, adding enough sugar to make Gino wince. Which was how it had been for decades.

"The same." Fear had kept Kayla silent in the days after her father was shot, but Charlotte's arm around her shoulders had given her the courage to tell Tino what she'd seen. "I thought Charlotte would pass out when she saw the sketch."

She hadn't passed out, but she'd gone numb. And silent. She hadn't said a word when Vito had come to her apartment to get Kayla's statement.

She hadn't said a word when Tino had packed up Mrs. Tripplehorn's food and litter box, stowing the cat in a carrier. Nor when he'd put the cat carrier and her suitcase in the back of his car and buckled her into his front passenger seat.

She hadn't even commented when he pulled into the driveway of the house he shared with Gino. He'd planned on going with her to the hotel she'd reserved, but he needed his home Wi-Fi connection for what he planned to do next.

Hotel Wi-Fi was not secure, and he didn't want anyone to know what he was doing—especially not Philly PD. What he needed was in the home office that he and Gino shared.

So the home office was where he went, with Gino trailing after him, sipping his own coffee. It was late for Gino. He was typically an early riser, where Tino was a night owl. They rarely shared the same space, which was probably why their living situation had been so successful for so long.

"Could you have been followed?" Gino asked.

Tino sat at his desk. "No. I drove all over the place before we came here. She just stared out the window like a zombie."

"I get it," Gino murmured. "She's blaming herself for the bloodshed. That can't be easy to accept."

"No," Tino agreed. He got it, too, and it was breaking his heart. So he'd tucked her into his bed where she could get some rest. Now he was doing something about this mess. "Oof," he grunted when Charlotte's cat jumped onto his lap.

It appeared that Mrs. Tripplehorn needed some comfort, too.

"We should get a cat of our own," Gino said as he pulled up a chair and sat beside Tino, looking at his computer screen. "What are you doing?"

"No, *we* should not get a cat. If we get one, it'll be yours. I travel too much to take care of a pet. And I'm helping Vito solve this thing," Tino said grimly as he stroked Mrs. Tripplehorn's back. "Hopefully he's already got someone in his department doing this, but I need to do something or I'll lose my mind."

Gino leaned closer, his brows lifting as he realized what Tino had begun. "How did you get such a realistic-looking photo from your sketch?"

"AI," Tino replied. "Easy to do. I already converted the sketch

I did from Mrs. Johnson's description and gave it to Nick Lawrence, but Kayla's description was sharper than Mrs. J.'s. I got a better sketch. Younger eyes, and Kayla wasn't being beaten up at the time like Mrs. Johnson was."

"How is Mrs. Johnson?"

"Improving. Still in the ICU, but hopefully they'll move her in the next day or two."

"That's really good to hear." He pointed to Tino's screen. "Does Vito have this photo?"

"Yep. Sent it to him before I left Charlotte's place. I'm able to render it into a photo on my phone, but for the next step, I need my desktop computer."

Gino tilted his head, frowning. "Maybe it's my imagination, but there's something about that guy that's familiar."

"I thought the same, but Charlotte didn't recognize him." That had been the last sentence he'd extracted from her before she'd gone silent. "She was in shock, though, so after some sleep, she might be able to look again."

"And now what are you doing?" Gino pressed.

"Facial recognition software." Tino set up the parameters to the program, then started the process.

"I didn't know that you knew how to do that."

"Learned from a tech guy who works for a PI. I got called in to do a sketch for one of their clients, and their tech guy matched the face with a name using facial recognition software. He showed me how to do a search of various databases to match my sketch to a person."

Gino narrowed his eyes. "Various databases? Which various databases?"

And this was why Tino had needed to come home to run this program. He had his internet routed through several proxy servers—another thing the PI's tech guy had taught him. He didn't want anyone to know which databases he had access to.

"You don't want to know."

"Was this tech guy a hacker?"

Tino smiled. "A really good one. I can check against mugshots and even DMV photos."

"And nobody's going to trace it back to our house, right?"

Tino gave him a look. "Would I put you in danger?"

"Yes," Gino said immediately. "You did it all the time when we were kids."

Tino snickered. "You were such a goody-goody. 'Oh no, Tino,'" he said in a falsetto, "'you're gonna get us in trouble.'"

"He wouldn't have been wrong," a voice said dryly from the office doorway.

Charlotte stood there, looking lost. But she was trying to rally.

Gino stood. "Charlotte. What can I get you?"

"That coffee smells good," she said. "Maybe a cup?"

Gino smiled at her gently. "Of course. Sit down. Take my chair."

She obeyed, taking the chair he'd vacated so she could see Tino's computer screen. "I always knew you'd be a bad boy. Hacking into databases, Tino? Really?"

Tino grinned. "Really." Then he sobered. "Are you okay?"

"No," she said honestly, then smiled up at Gino when he gave her a cup of coffee. "Thank you. And thank you for letting us invade your space. Even Mrs. Tripplehorn."

Gino laughed, taking the cat from Tino and cuddling her up against his chest. "She's a nice cat."

Charlotte rolled her eyes. "She's nice to you two. She's a monster to everyone else. She only tolerates me because I feed her." She sipped at the coffee, returning her gaze to Tino's screen. "Tell me that we aren't breaking any laws?"

Tino waggled his hand back and forth. "Maybe one or two."

"Tino," Charlotte sighed. "Vito's going to be doing this, too, you know. Why risk it?"

"Because I can be faster, and because he might not be able to share with us whatever he finds. His goal is to catch a killer. My goal is to keep you safe. Period, full stop. I want to know who we're dealing with."

Her eyes filled with gratitude. "How long does it take?"

"Could take all night. Could be hours or even minutes." The laptop dinged loudly. "Or it could be now." Tino tapped his keyboard and heard Charlotte's indrawn breath at the mugshot that filled his screen. "This was faster because this guy served time locally. I started with the local law enforcement databases."

Gino pulled up another chair. "Kevin Hale," he murmured, reading the screen.

"Served time for armed robbery," Tino said. "Arrested at eighteen and served nine years of his fourteen-year sentence. Was out for less than a year before he got locked up again for another robbery. This time he served the full fourteen. Got out less than a month ago."

"He robbed a liquor store the first time and then a corner store the second time," Gino said. "And now he's allegedly robbed a pizza place, another corner store, and a dry cleaner's. At least he's consistent. He could have stepped up and robbed a bank."

"The bank didn't have Charlotte's address," Tino said lightly, then noticed a detail that had his full attention. "Look at *his* past addresses. When he was arrested the first time, he lived in our old neighborhood. The second time, too. He must have moved back home after getting out."

Charlotte reached for the mouse with a trembling hand, scrolling down the screen to see more of Kevin Hale's biographical information. "Oh my God. Tino. He went to our high school."

Tino clicked a link, bringing up the man's first mugshot, taken twenty-three years ago. But he still didn't recognize him.

Gino snapped his fingers. "*That's* why he looks familiar. I graduated with that guy. He would have been a year behind you guys. He was in my shop class. Kind of a loner, as I recall."

Tino frowned. Charlotte was even paler than she'd been before. Her hand covered her mouth, and her eyes were wide and haunted. "Charlotte? What's wrong?" He tugged her hand from her mouth when she didn't answer right away. "Charlie?"

The old nickname got her attention, and she drew a deep breath. "I tutored him, Tino. In history. To get my volunteer hours for my college applications. I didn't remember."

"Why would you?" Tino asked, keeping his tone soothing. He still held her hand and didn't want to let it go. "What do you remember now?"

She swallowed hard. "He was a loner, but he . . . liked me."

"Everyone liked you, Charlotte," Tino said. "You were one of the popular girls." He'd been a popular guy, and together they'd been high school royalty. Prom king and queen. Then what she'd said fully registered. "He liked you or he *liked* you?"

"The second one," she said quietly. "He asked me to prom. I . . . I wanted to let him down easy because he seemed so lonely. I didn't want to hurt his feelings."

"What did you tell him?" Gino asked.

"That I'd already agreed to go with Tino, but that if I hadn't had a steady boyfriend, that I would have gone with him. I mean, I knew I'd go to senior prom with Tino back in the ninth grade when I first met him, but this guy didn't know that."

Tino squeezed her hand. "I knew the same. So, have you heard from him since high school?"

She shook her head, then sucked in another harsh breath. "Oh my God. What prison was he in?" She leaned closer to the screen to read the answer and her whole body stilled. "Oh my God."

"Charlie," Tino murmured, and she met his gaze, hers filled with tears. "Did he contact you?"

"Someone did. I got emails for a while saying that a prisoner wanted to email with me. I just deleted them."

"When did they start?" Tino asked, pulling out his phone. He was going to have to call Vito with this information ASAP.

Charlotte sat back in her chair, her whole body trembling.

Tino set his phone on the table and put his arms around her. "Hey," he whispered. "Talk to me."

"It's my fault. Dottie and Mr. Lombardi and Mrs. Fadil. Mr. Lewis. They're all on me."

"No," Tino said firmly. "They are on Kevin Hale, if he's the one who did this. You are a good person, Charlotte Walsh. You would never hurt anyone. Not knowingly."

She pressed her face into his neck, and Tino immediately felt the moisture from her tears. "I hurt you."

He stroked her hair, remembering all the times he'd done so in their past. "Breaking an eighteen-year-old kid's heart because you don't want the same things out of life is not the same thing as assault and murder. Not even in the same universe. You know this, Charlie."

She shuddered in his arms and began to sob. "You called me Charlie again. Three times."

"Should I not?"

"No, no. Please. I . . . needed that. Needed to know you still see me."

"I've always seen you," Tino whispered.

"No. *See* me like you did before. Before I broke your heart."

This was why he'd steadfastly called her Charlotte. "I've always seen you," he repeated, because it was true.

Because he was helpless to stop himself from falling for her all over again.

She slid her arms around his neck and held on. Watching as Gino slipped out of the room, Tino rubbed her back, letting her cry it all out. Sometimes a person just needed a good, cathartic cry.

Finally, the sobs slowed to hiccups and she sagged against him wearily. "I'm sorry."

He tightened his hold. She was sturdier now than she'd been at eighteen, her shoulders rounder, her figure curvier. But she was far more fragile at the same time. "Hush. No saying you're sorry. Not to me."

She pulled away and he missed the feel of her in his arms.

Gino was a hero and was ready with a cold cloth for her swollen eyes. "We've got bags of frozen peas if you need something colder."

She laughed wetly. "The cloth will be fine, thank you." She took a moment to collect herself. "The emails started when I was in college. I kept the email address I had in high school for a few years."

"When did you get rid of it?" Tino asked.

"The summer between my sophomore and junior year, when my parents got divorced and sold the house. Canceled the internet. My email address was attached to their cable service." She met Tino's eyes again. "But I think it was more that I was hoping you'd contact me."

Tino felt sucker punched. "You told me not to."

"I know. I thought it would be easier."

"For who?" Tino asked, acutely aware that his brother wasn't even pretending not to listen.

"I said it was for you, but I think it was more for me. If you'd asked me to come home, I probably would have. And I wasn't ready yet."

Tino didn't understand, but this wasn't the time for the conversation they desperately needed to have. "All right. The emails from the prison system started in college."

She flinched at his brusque topic change but nodded. "My freshman year. I just kept deleting them, thinking that everyone got them. Finally, after two years of it, I told my RA—my resident advisor—and she told me to change my email address. I had one at school that classmates and teachers used and my folks weren't big emailers. They preferred to call me on the phone. That was right about the time they got divorced and sold the house. They both moved. Mom went to Jersey and Dad went to Michigan."

"Why were they together when they died?" Tino asked, then wished he hadn't when her eyes filled with pain.

"They were coming to see me. It was after the car accident I had with my ex, which caused the injuries that made me need the cane. Mom and Dad flew in on different flights and met up at the airport. They were in a rental car and got hit by a semi that was dodging a car that zipped in front of it."

"Oh, Charlie," Tino murmured. "You felt guilty, didn't you?"

"Surprisingly, no. The driver of the car who did the stupid move in front of the semi was charged. I had someone else to blame besides myself. This is different, though, Tino. This guy yelled 'Where is she?' right before he shot Mr. Lewis. Kayla thought he was looking for her, but we both know he was looking for me. *Me*, Tino."

Tino nodded. "I'm certain he was looking for you." And he was so glad that the asshole hadn't known Charlotte's home address. "But that still doesn't make it your fault. Were you kind to Kevin Hale back in high school?"

"Yes, but no more kind than I was to anyone else who wasn't you. He must have thought I meant it personally."

"See?" Tino said. "Not your fault. You were kind, Charlotte.

You didn't lead him on. That wasn't your way. If he's obsessed with you—and it sounds like that's what's happening here—it's on him. Not you." He could see that he wasn't getting through, so he let it go for now. "Let's call Vito and bring him up to date."

And then Tino would get busy finding out everything there was to know about Kevin Hale.

"How are you going to explain the facial recognition software and access to databases you shouldn't know how to get into?" she asked. "Because Vito will ask."

He glanced at Gino. "I could tell him that Gino recognized him from school."

"Not a total lie," Gino said cheerfully. "I'll be a fucking hero."

Charlotte smiled at Gino before turning back to Tino. "Then let's call Vito."

CHAPTER 6

Vito looked at Gino across Tino's dining room table. Vito had come as soon as he'd found someone to sit with Sophie and now appeared highly skeptical of Tino's explanation of how they'd gotten Kevin Hale's name, which Charlotte found to be no surprise. But she kept her mouth shut because Tino had done this for her. She wasn't going to get him into any more trouble.

"You recognized him, huh?" Vito said, brows raised.

Gino nodded vigorously. "From Tino's photo rendition of his sketch. Kevin Hale was in my shop class. We sat near each other, and I helped him with his senior project."

"I see," Vito said dryly, clearly not buying Gino's explanation. "Did he ever mention Charlotte back then?"

Beside her, Tino relaxed a fraction. Vito might not have entirely believed Gino, but it didn't seem like he was making a big deal about it.

"No," Gino said. "Not that I remember. He didn't say much of anything. Kind of a loner. He got easily distracted, I do remember that. Cut the tip of his finger off one day on a band saw. That's when the teacher assigned me to him. I was supposed to keep him from chopping off anything else. But we didn't talk much."

"Did he want to do woodworking?" Vito asked. "Or was he just taking the class for a random credit?"

Gino pursed his lips, thinking. "I think he wanted to learn to build things. When he did talk, he mentioned building a house someday. In the burbs with a picket fence. He'd have a family. I'd forgotten that."

"That's good," Vito said. "He ever mention anyone he wanted that family with?"

Gino thought some more then slowly nodded. "Said he had her all picked out. But he never mentioned Charlotte. I'd have picked up on that, if only because we were all mad at her at that point for breaking Tino's heart."

Charlotte fought the urge to wince. It was true. She had done that.

But Tino had called her Charlie. He'd held her like he cared. And even if they never got back what they'd had, maybe he could actually forgive her someday.

It wasn't what she really wanted, but she'd lost her chance at that. Tino had offered her a family, but she'd thrown it away because she wanted adventure. She'd wanted independence. She'd been afraid of tying herself down to one person, even though she'd loved him.

She'd been a fool.

But you were young. You didn't know.

No, she hadn't known what she was losing the day she walked away.

Except that she *had* known. She'd thought she'd get over the loss, but she'd been so wrong. Young, foolish, and wrong.

She'd blown her chance, but he'd called her Charlie and that would be enough.

"Charlotte?" Vito said loudly, like he'd called her name a few times already.

She blinked. "I'm sorry. My mind is . . ." She rubbed her temples. "I got lost in my head. What was that again?"

"I asked about the emails you received from the prison. Didn't you open them to see the name of the inmate who wanted to talk to you?"

She sighed. "This is going to sound vacuous and awful, but I forgot about Kevin five minutes after our last tutoring session. Never gave him another thought until tonight. If I saw his name in one of those emails, I wouldn't have recognized it. I was away from home for the first time and going to parties and all that. I had to have opened the first email, but I just deleted the rest." She grimaced. "And that wasn't the name I thought of when I saw him, anyway."

"What name did you think of?" Tino asked.

"Simon." She was surprised to see both Vito and Tino flinch, like that name hurt them, and then she remembered that their Simon had been a vicious killer. "Like the chipmunk. His voice was very high. I almost called him that once but caught myself in time."

"No one has mentioned a high-pitched voice," Vito said thoughtfully. "It might be lower now that he's older, but it's worth asking Kayla. What else do you remember about him?"

"He always brought me flowers. Every time we had a tutoring session. I always took them by Aunt Dottie's classroom. She loves flowers." A new memory surfaced, and she sucked in a breath. "He saw them there once. He asked me why I'd given the flowers away. He was really mad. Made me a little nervous. He was taller than me. Skinny as a pole, but I guess he bulked up."

"A lot of guys do while they're in prison," Vito said. "What did you tell him about the flowers?"

"I lied. I told him I had terrible allergies, but I didn't want his gift to go to waste, which was why I gave them to my aunt. He seemed to accept that and calmed down."

"How might he have gotten your email address?" Vito asked.

"I gave it to him so we could arrange tutoring sessions. It seemed wiser at the time than giving him my phone number."

"It probably was," Vito said. "And now we know how he knew to hang out at your aunt's house, waiting for you. But if he did that, why wouldn't he have just followed you home? Why go to Lombardi's to get your address?"

Charlotte rubbed her temples again. "Most of the time I didn't go straight home. I'd always get a late dinner after seeing Dottie. She eats dinner at, like, five o'clock, and she isn't as adventurous with food as she used to be. Meat and potatoes are her thing. I'd be hungry again by the time I left and wanting to eat something more interesting, so I'd try different restaurants. But even if I was going straight home, I never drove straight there. I'm in the habit of driving around before I go home so that no one follows me. Part of the paranoia since the attack."

"Understandable," Vito said quietly. "Don't be ashamed of habits that help you feel safer. You might have saved your own life."

"But lost Mr. Lombardi and Mrs. Fadil theirs," she said bitterly.

"I'm not going to tell you that it's not your fault," Vito said, "because folks in your position are never ready to hear it. I will recommend a good therapist."

"I have one of those, but thank you anyway." Her therapist was going to have a field day with all of this. She'd almost convinced Charlotte that there was nothing to fear.

Hahaha.

Vito smiled. "Okay. I'll give Tino the therapist's name in case you change your mind. Now, next question. How did he know you were back in town? You never told anyone in Memphis where you were going and you've done a very good job at covering your tracks. I had a hard time getting through the company you set up for your condo purchase, and I tried very hard."

"At least I did something right."

"You've done a lot of things right," Tino said loyally.

Charlotte patted his hand. "And you're being kind. I don't know how he knew I was back in town. Could it have been a chance passing on the street?"

"Always a possibility," Vito allowed. "But you eat out a lot, right?"

"For my job, yes. But I don't review restaurants in Philly. I eat out here only if I've eaten at Dottie's. If I'm not at Dottie's, I cook at home."

Vito tapped his tablet and turned it so she could see the screen. "Ever eat at any of these places?"

Charlotte scanned the list. "Only one. The sushi place. Why?"

"When?" Vito pressed.

Mentally she counted days. "Ten days ago. It was on Saturday night. I'd taken Dottie to the annual flower show and then we watched reruns on TV until she fell asleep. I was famished, and I'd heard good things about the place, so I went. Why?"

"Did you eat in or take out?"

"Ate in." She scowled at him. "*Why?*"

"Because Kevin Hale worked there until ten days ago."

Tino visibly startled. "How do you know that?"

"When you called me and told me Hale's name, I called the warden where he served his time. He said that Kevin had said that he gotten a job at this sushi restaurant. I went there to speak to the owner before I came here," Vito explained. "Hale was a waiter, but he got fired after walking out of the Saturday night rush. Offered no explanation. Just walked out."

Bile rose to burn Charlotte's throat. "He saw me there."

"I think so," Vito said. "Breathe, Charlotte. You're looking awfully pale."

Beside her, Tino took her hand and squeezed. "We'll figure this out," he promised.

She wanted so much to believe him. "Two people are dead and two others are in critical condition because I wanted sushi."

Vito shook his head patiently. "No. It's because Kevin Hale is mentally ill."

Her eyes widened. "Clinically?"

"Yep. The warden said he was a sociopath who struggled with delusions while he was serving his sentence. The warden also said he was a loner except for the guy he shared a cell with. I'm going to see the cellmate myself tomorrow."

"I want to go," Tino said.

Vito shook his head. "Don't ask me, Tino."

"I'm asking. I've done everything you've ever asked me to do. I've listened to victims recount their worst nightmares time and time again so that they could get justice. I've helped your department so many times. Now I'm asking you for a favor. Take me with you."

Vito sighed. "I'll think about it, okay?"

Tino shook his head stubbornly. "No. Not okay. I'm going. And if you tell me no, I'll figure out how to go myself."

Vito closed his eyes briefly. "Tino."

"He screams at night," Gino said quietly. "Nightmares. That's when he sleeps. Sometimes I swear he doesn't sleep for days. Yet he still goes wherever the victims are, whenever you or anyone else asks. Don't tell him no, Vito. Let him go. He doesn't ask for much."

Charlotte hadn't considered the toll Tino's work might take on him emotionally, but it wasn't really a surprise. She'd sensed a heaviness to his spirit when they'd first seen each other in Dottie's hospital room and again when he'd worked with Kayla, walking her through what had been the worst experience of her young life. That had to weigh him down.

Vito sighed again. "You guys are ganging up on me."

"Yes," Gino said. "We are."

Vito rolled his eyes. "You can go. But not you, Charlotte."

Charlotte shuddered in relief. "That's okay. I don't want to go."

"Someone has common sense," Vito muttered. "I don't know what you're expecting to hear or learn, Tino. The cellmate might not know anything. He might clam up or ask for considerations I'm not willing—or able—to provide. The DA's not going to want to deal with this guy. He's in for murder."

"I don't know either," Tino said. "But I know I need to be there. Thank you."

"Don't make me regret it. I'll leave as soon as I get the kids off to school. Tomorrow's going to be the last day I have to juggle. Tess is flying in tomorrow to stay with us until the baby comes. She's bringing the twins, so Dad is coming over during the day to babysit. My house is going to be Grand Central for the next few weeks, assuming Sophie makes it to forty weeks. I'm hoping for the full four weeks of craziness."

"I can help, too," Charlotte offered. "When I'm not with Aunt Dottie at the hospital, I can run errands."

Vito's smile was a little too sharp. "Thank you, but you're going to a safe house."

Charlotte shook her head. "I can't. Dottie needs me."

"Your aunt needs you *alive*," Vito insisted.

"We'll stay with her," Gino offered unexpectedly. "Tino mostly, but I can stay when he's off to the prison tomorrow." He grinned at Tino. "So many people thought you'd eventually do time. Now you will."

Tino laughed. "Fuck off, asshole." He sobered. "And thank you."

Charlotte wanted to deny that she needed a full-time babysitter, but she was no fool. Not anymore. "Yes, Gino. Thank you."

* * *

MOUNT AIRY, PHILADELPHIA, PENNSYLVANIA
THURSDAY, MARCH 31, 1:20 A.M.

"CAN I GET YOU ANYTHING?" Tino asked, standing in his bedroom doorway.

Charlotte sat on the edge of the bed, looking so lost. She lifted her eyes to his and his heart hurt at the misery she carried.

"No," she said quietly. "You've given me a safe place to sleep. That's all I can ask for."

He took a step forward, then stopped himself. She needed space to process. He got that. But he didn't want to give her space. He wanted to wrap his arms around her and hold her tight. Wanted her to feel the beat of his heart.

Wanted her to know that he cared.

A lot.

She swallowed. "You don't have to stay. I know you're tired, too."

There was a wistfulness in her tone.

"Do you want me to stay?" he asked, unable to keep his voice smooth and neutral. The words had come out husky and full of emotion.

Because he wanted to stay. Wanted to hold her every bit as much for himself as for her. He wanted to feel the beat of her heart, too.

"Would that be okay? I'm not expecting anything, Tino. I promise."

What if I want you to expect something?

The words were on the tip of his tongue but he bit them back. Not now. Not when she was vulnerable and hurting.

"Let me change into some sweats." He pointed to the door behind her. "En suite bathroom is through there. Take your time. I won't leave."

Relief shimmered through her eyes. He'd said the right thing.

He'd be whatever she needed him to be tonight.

And tomorrow?

Tomorrow, too. She was back in his life, a gift he hadn't known he'd longed for. But he had.

She disappeared into the bathroom and Tino raced to change his clothes. He had to rifle through his dresser drawers because sweatpants and a T-shirt weren't his normal sleeping attire.

Normally he slept in the buff. But not tonight.

And if that's what she wants?

Nope. Not gonna go there.

But it was too late. His body already had gone there. He was hard and wanting and in a few minutes he'd hold her in his arms. In his bed.

No. He stared down at his erection, willing it to subside. He made himself think of gross things—bags full of garbage on the city streets in August. No, not bad enough. He was still raring to go.

How about that time his nephew Dominic had beer for the

first time on his twenty-first birthday and threw up all over Tino's shoes?

He grimaced, remembering having to throw the shoes away. Yeah, that took care of the erection.

He'd really liked those shoes, too.

The bathroom door opened, revealing Charlotte in clothing similar to his own. "Why do you look so disgusted?" she asked. "My sweats are clean."

Tino chuckled. "It's not you. I promise."

She gave him an odd look. "Okay." Nervously she eyed the bed. "Is it okay if I . . . ?"

"Of course." He pulled back the blanket, gesturing for her to get between the sheets, his heart pounding harder as she did so. He joined her, turning off the light and pulling the blankets over them snugly. It was supposed to be cold tonight, but his body was burning up.

Not a fever.

Just desire. Want. He gritted his teeth, willing his body to behave. But her presence in his bed took him back twenty-four years. Back to when they'd been young and reckless. Back to the first time they'd had sex. He'd lain awake afterward for hours, just watching her and marveling that she was his.

Could she be again? He was terrified to hope.

Charlotte lifted her head off the pillow. "It's okay, Tino. I'll sleep on the sofa. You take the bed."

"No." He rolled to his side to frown at her. "Why?"

"Because you're so tense about being here. About sharing a bed with me."

Tino sighed. "Well, I am, but clearly not for the reasons you're assuming. Charlotte, you're . . . well, you're a beautiful woman. And I'm only human."

Her eyes widened, and then her lips curved, surprising him. "Really?"

She sounded delighted.

He laughed. "Really. But I'm not eighteen anymore. I can control myself." He sobered when her smile dimmed. "Charlotte, I'll stay here with you. You are worth any discomfort."

She exhaled quietly. "Thank you, Tino. I don't deserve your kindness, but I'm so grateful for it."

"Hush. You deserve kindness." On an impulse, he held his arm wide. "Come here. Let me hold you. Maybe it'll help both of us sleep."

She moved closer until her head was on his shoulder, her hand on his chest, her body burrowing into his side. She was soft and warm, and she smelled like lemons. Her murmur of contentment made something within him settle.

He hadn't been able to hold her like this often when they'd been young. Their parents had been eagle-eyed, not giving them opportunities to "get into trouble."

Of course, their parents hadn't known everything. They'd had a few stolen moments, holding each other just like this. Those, however, had usually been preceded by sex.

Which he was not going to think about. He was going to enjoy holding her until sleep took him and then he'd wake up and go to the prison with Vito to get some answers about Kevin Hale and the nature of his endgame.

"I felt like I was going to suffocate," Charlotte murmured, completely out of the blue.

Tino tightened his hold on her. "What? When? Now?"

"No. When I was eighteen."

Ah. This would be the explanation he'd been hoping for. He considered turning on a light, but it might be easier for her to explain in the dark.

It might be easier for him to hear, too.

"Why?"

She sighed, her breath warm against his shoulder. "My

parents fought all the time when I was in high school. Dad hit my mother once. They stayed together for me. I'd lie awake at night and hear them screaming at each other, and it was awful."

"I didn't know it was that bad." His own parents' relationship had been okay at that point in his life. His mother had been critical of all her children, but if his parents had fought back then, he hadn't known about it. It wasn't until later that they'd discovered the lies his mother had told. Their family had never been the same afterward.

"It was. When they divorced a few years after I left for college, I was kind of relieved. I found ways not to visit home on the holidays. I mostly went home with friends. Anything to avoid my folks."

"I don't understand why you felt like you were suffocating."

She was quiet for a moment. "I don't know how to explain it. It's just that every time I thought about marriage, I'd get anxious. I didn't want marriage. I didn't want what they had, being stuck together while hating each other. My mother would scream at him that she could have had a career if he hadn't knocked her up. With me. She wanted to be a dancer, but she had to give that up when I came along. Then she was married and living in a house with a white picket fence and having meatloaf on Wednesdays."

Which was what Tino had told her he'd wanted for their life together. "You didn't want to be trapped with me."

"*No.* I wanted to be with you. But I was afraid that if I let myself have that, that I'd become my mother. You wanted babies right away and . . . I didn't. I wanted to experience independence. My mother moved from her parents' house right into my father's house and she hated him for that. I loved you so much, but I was afraid of the life that you said you wanted."

"I would have let you do whatever you wanted," Tino said, then grimaced. "That came out wrong. I wouldn't have *let* you do anything. You could have made the rules, and I would have done whatever you wanted. I just wanted you."

"I know. But I still wanted to be on my own, for a little while. I look back now and see how foolish I was. I gave you up for what I thought was my dream, and I missed you from the moment I walked away."

"But you couldn't change your mind," Tino said, hoping he understood and trying not to take her words too personally. "Because then you'd be trapped."

"I guess. Like I said, I can't explain it well."

"Could you breathe? After you left?"

"Yes," she said quietly, and he had to draw a deep breath because the single word hurt him. "But it didn't last long. There were responsibilities wherever I went. Always someone who needed something. Friends, teachers. My parents. I thought I'd be free and everything would be easy when I was on my own, and in some ways, I *was* free, but . . . I missed you. I hated myself for hurting you."

"Why didn't you tell me how you felt?"

"Because you were Tino Ciccotelli. You were prom king."

"You were prom queen."

"I was a dinghy, floating in your wake."

He flinched then. He couldn't help it. "Oh."

She patted his chest. "I had no self-confidence then, Tino. I pretended. I was always pretending. I pretended my home life was happy, that I had it together. That I was up and bubbly and a cheerleader and all the things I was supposed to be. I thought if I had to pretend for another second that I'd crack into pieces."

He held his tongue for a long moment, trying to get his words organized. Because this was a critical moment and he didn't want to fuck it up. "Were you pretending with me? When you said you loved me?"

"No. That was maybe the only honest thing I did say."

"You realize we were all pretending, right?"

She lifted her head to stare at him. "What?"

"I was self-conscious, too. I was Tino, but you were Charlotte. Charlie. Everyone wanted to be with you and I wondered why you'd chosen me. But we were teenagers. We all pretended to some extent."

"I don't think it's the same."

"Maybe not. And you felt how you felt. I just wish you'd told me."

"I didn't know how. And I hated myself for that, too."

He ran a hand over her hair, soothing her and himself, too. "I didn't know."

"I didn't want you to. I'd pretended for so long that telling you was too terrifying. I didn't want to hurt you, but I did anyway."

"You did," he agreed. "But I lived. So did you."

"I was stupid."

"You were eighteen. We were all a little stupid."

"I figured you'd meet someone else and get your house with a picket fence and meatloaf on Wednesdays."

"I didn't. No one was you."

She inhaled sharply. "Tino."

"Shh. It's okay. We're here now."

"I'm broken now."

No. He wasn't going to let her say that about herself. "You're stronger now. Do you still pretend?"

"Sometimes. Every time I went to a restaurant in disguise I was pretending, but that was . . . fun."

"What about with your ex? Did you pretend with him?"

She said nothing for several hard beats of his heart. Then she made a thoughtful noise that vibrated against his skin. "No. When he wanted me to be a quiet wife who let him cheat, I left him."

"Good. Do you still feel like a dinghy in anyone's wake?"

"Not recently."

"Good."

"Do you pretend?" she asked.

"Yes." The word snapped out of his mouth before he could stop it.

"With me?"

"Yes," he said more gently. "I've pretended that we were just friends and I don't think that's true. At least I don't want it to be. But I didn't want to frighten you off, and if we're being totally honest here, I didn't want to risk my heart with you again."

"Same," she whispered. "What can we do?"

He hesitated, considering his answer. "What do you want to happen, Charlotte?"

"I'd like to hear you call me Charlie."

He swallowed thickly. "Charlie."

She shuddered out a breath. "Thank you."

"You're welcome. What else?"

"I'd like to see you. Date you. Like normal people who don't have a crazed killer after them."

He chuckled. "Okay. We should go on more dates."

"More?"

He scoffed. "Like I haven't taken you on a few already."

"I'd hoped they were dates," she said softly. "I don't want to hurt you again."

"You probably will. I'll probably hurt you. But we'll talk about it, Charlie. No running away."

"I promise. Can . . . can I kiss you?"

"Yes," he whispered and held his breath.

She rose up on her elbow and brushed her lips over his. He closed his eyes and let himself feel. She was with him again after so long, and while he still didn't completely understand why she'd left, he wasn't going to squander this second chance they'd been given.

Her lips were soft, then firmer as she increased the pressure.

His pulse skyrocketed to the moon when she lightly licked his lips, and what had been a chaste kiss exploded into so much more. He slid one hand to the back of her neck, pulling her closer, moaning into her mouth when her fingers tightened in his hair.

Her hips rolled against his leg and he couldn't resist her, his free hand running up her side, under the shirt she wore. Touching her soft skin. "God, I want you," he murmured when she finally lifted her head, both of them breathing fast. "I've been hard for two days."

She chuckled, a deep and wicked sound. "And I've been wet. Show me, Tino."

He rolled, reversing their positions so that he looked down at her. "What do you want? I need you to be specific." She bit at her lip and he tugged it free of her teeth. "Don't be shy now, Charlie. Tell me what you want."

"I want you to . . ." She closed her eyes. "Are you really going to make me say it?"

"Yes," he said seriously. "I need the words."

She opened her eyes, and even in the semidarkness, he could see her determination. "I want you to make love to me."

He exhaled, glad that he was lying down because he was certain his knees would have buckled had he been standing. "I don't have condoms."

"Yes, you do." She rolled sideways to open his nightstand drawer, pulling out a strip of three condoms.

Condoms that had not been there earlier that day.

"Did you bring them?" he asked.

She blinked up at him. "No. Remember, I asked you for

Tylenol when we first got here tonight, and you said to check the drawer. The condoms were just . . . there."

Gino. His brother had to have put them there. It was the only explanation. "I haven't been with anyone in a long time, Charlie. At least two years. And never here. Not in this bed." He usually found women when he was traveling out of town, lonely women who knew he wouldn't be coming back. He'd never lead them on. Anything else would have been cruel. "Those aren't mine."

Her lips curved in satisfaction. "Then I guess we'll thank the condom fairies tomorrow."

He chuckled. "Not on your life." He rested his forehead against hers, the gravity of the moment sinking in. She was in his arms. In his bed. "I've missed you. So much."

"Same," she whispered. "Show me how much."

So he did, kissing her until she was once again rolling her hips against him. He leaned over and turned on the light. "I want to see you."

She opened her mouth, then closed it on a sigh. "No, you don't."

He wanted to insist, but she'd gone from passionate to miserable. "Why not?"

"I have scars. They're not pretty. He . . . he cut me."

Scars. Her attacker had cut her with her own knives. A part of him wanted to say fine, he'd turn off the light, but this was a big deal. "We said we'd communicate. Your scars won't bother me. Your wrinkles won't bother me."

"I don't have wrinkles," she asserted, sounding mildly aggrieved.

That made him smile. "I do. I don't care that we're both forty-two years old. I'm not the boy you knew, Charlie. I'm older and not as toned as I used to be. But I'm here and so are you. You said you wanted me to *see* you. Let me do that. Let me see all of you."

She nodded then. "Okay. Start as we mean to continue, yes?"

"Yes." He kissed her until she was writhing against him once again. When she was panting and making the sweetest little sounds, he pulled her shirt over her head. And stared.

"You're so beautiful," he murmured. And she was. Her breasts were fuller, her curves rounder. There were scars, yes. But not so many as he'd feared. He wanted to kill the man who'd put them there, but the bastard was already dead. He shoved his rage down, choosing to be in the moment. To be with her. "So beautiful."

"You make me believe that," she murmured back. "Your clothes, too." She yanked his T-shirt over his head and tossed it to the floor. Humming, she ran her hands up his arms, caressing his biceps and his shoulders. "I dreamed of this last night. Dreamed of you."

The rest of their clothes seemed to disappear, and then he was rolling a condom over his erection and sliding inside her.

It was like coming home. Everything felt so damn right.

He watched her as he began to move, cataloging every sigh, every hitch of her breath so that he knew how to make her feel amazing. And when she finally came, quietly chanting his name, he felt like a god.

His own release rushed over him in a wave from which he never wanted to surface. But eventually his heart began to slow and he rolled to his side, taking her with him. For long, lovely moments they just lay there, breathing in sync with each another.

He kissed her forehead. "I'll be right back." He went to the bathroom and dealt with the condom, then came back to a warm bed and a satisfied woman. She returned to his arms, her head once again resting on his shoulder.

"Thank you," she murmured. "That was perfect."

"It really was."

She pulled away to look down at him. "For real?"

"For real. No more pretending, Charlie. For either of us."

She settled back against his shoulder. "Good night, Tino."

"Good night, Charlie."

CHAPTER 7

"His last known address was a dead end," Vito said as he drove them to the prison. "Kevin Hale was released from prison and just disappeared."

They'd been quiet for most of the drive, Vito deep in thought. As was Tino, although he might have dozed for part of the way. He'd held Charlotte all night, finally falling asleep shortly before dawn. His eyes felt like sandpaper.

"No parole officer," Tino muttered.

"Nope. He served his full sentence. He has an aging grandmother and gave his address as her home, but she says he's never been there. That she would not have welcomed him into her house. Her neighbors corroborated this, saying that they'd seen no one entering or exiting in the past six months other than the Meals on Wheels delivery person and her home health-care nurse. Both women. No men have been seen around her house."

"He could have snuck in."

"Possibly, but he's not there now. The grandmother claims not to have known he'd finished serving his sentence. She was a little forgetful, but she was firm on that point. There was no evidence of anyone else having been in the house, and she allowed us to search. I think she was afraid Hale had broken in and really was living upstairs. She's confined to the lower floor of her house now. The upper level hadn't been disturbed in quite some time."

"When did your detectives search her house?" Tino asked.

"We went last night, after I met with you and Charlotte. I searched the place myself, Tino. I wanted to be sure for you."

Tino reached across the console and gripped Vito's arm. "Thank you."

"It's the least I could do." He drew a breath. "Why didn't you tell me you were having nightmares?"

Tino shrugged. "I figured everyone did. Don't you?"

"Sometimes, but it's usually only the most intense cases. Children, mostly. Or if someone was brutally killed. Those are hard images to wipe." Vito sighed. "Sophie said she'd hit me if she were allowed to exert herself. She's known for a while that your job was wearing on you. She said she tried to tell me, but it never sunk in, I guess."

But of course Sophie had known. He and Sophie had been close ever since she'd entered Vito's life.

"She said it was wearing on me?"

"She actually said it was sucking out your soul."

Tino chuckled. That sounded more like Sophie. "It's not bad all the time, but I hear their stories and I feel so impotent. At least you can catch the bastards who hurt the people I've talked to."

"Because you tell us who to look for. Tino, your work is beyond important. But if it's sucking out your soul, you should stop."

"I've considered it from time to time, but never seriously. It's become more like a . . . calling, I suppose. Not just a job."

"I feel the same way about my job," Vito admitted. "Have you seen a therapist?"

"Yes. It's been a few years, but he helped. If it gets bad again, I'll go back."

"Do me a favor and go soon. Don't wait until it gets bad. It's just like with a wound. You gotta stay ahead of the pain."

Tino's eyes widened in surprise at the knowing in Vito's voice. "You?"

Vito's smile was wry. "Yes, me. I'd come home from work too tense, and it was impacting Sophie and the kids. So I talked to a therapist. For them, at first, but then I did it for me. It helped so much that I kept it up. I see mine every month like clockwork." He tapped his fingers on the steering wheel, clearly uncomfortable talking about his therapy. "So . . . you and Charlotte?"

Tino blushed like a teenager. "I hope so."

"Did she tell you why she left?"

"Yeah. I can't say that I totally understood, but it wasn't to hurt me. I am positive of that. We're going to try. Maybe see what happens."

"It's always been her, hasn't it?"

"Yes," Tino said simply.

"Which is why you've been alone all this time."

"Pretty much."

"Is that why you broke off your engagement all those years ago?"

"Actually, she broke it off with me. She realized that I wasn't fully committed and that we'd be better friends."

"Did she know about Charlotte?"

"Not by name, but I was honest with her. Told her that I hadn't gotten over my first love. She figured as much and told me she deserved better than a man who didn't love her completely. She was right. We're still friends, Vito. That breakup didn't break my heart."

"Good. I've worried about you all this time." Then Vito frowned. "What about Gino? Why is he still single then? Did someone break his heart, too?"

"I think he genuinely enjoys playing the field. He's not opposed to settling down. He just hasn't met anyone he wants to settle down with." Tino watched as the prison gates came into view. "Do you think this guy will be cooperative? Kevin Hale's cellmate?"

"He's a lifer. We can't offer him any time off his sentence, but he does have a daughter who lives in Harrisburg. The DA says we can offer him a transfer so that she can visit him more often."

Some of the tension in Tino's chest loosened. "You called the DA?"

"Of course I did. I woke him up after I left your house last night. I want to find Kevin Hale. He's hurt too many people. Too many families. I want him off the streets. So does the DA."

"Did the owner of the sushi restaurant where he worked tell you anything that might help?"

"Only that he'd taken a chance on hiring Hale as a busboy and had been pleased with his work ethic up until the time he disappeared from his shift without a word. This restaurant owner hires ex-cons, said Hale told him that one of the guys he'd known in prison had gotten out and gotten a job with him. Recommended Hale apply."

"Did he have the guy's name?" Tino asked, suddenly hopeful. "Could Hale be staying with the other ex-con?"

Vito hesitated, then shook his head. "Hale may have stayed with him at one point since his release, but he wasn't there, either."

There was something Vito wasn't saying, and Tino was

afraid he knew what that was. "What happened to that other ex-con?"

Vito sighed. "His name was Oscar Dupree. He's dead. The owner of the sushi place said that Dupree hadn't been in to work in a few days. We went to the address and found his body. Bullet through his head."

Tino's stomach twisted. "Dammit," he whispered.

"Yeah. Dupree's laptop was gone and a wall safe was empty, door hanging open. The victim's girlfriend said that he'd kept a lot of cash in the safe, just in case he had to leave town quickly. He served time for running drugs for a gang, and he's been looking over his shoulder since his release."

"So Hale might not have killed him."

"Maybe not, but the bullet that killed the guy was the same caliber as the one that killed Lombardi and Fadil and put Lewis in the hospital. The bullet's with Ballistics right now. Hopefully we'll have a definitive answer quickly."

"Why didn't he shoot Mrs. Johnson?" Tino asked, because he'd been wondering about that.

"He may have intended to. Someone two blocks away had a heart attack that night and called 911. Security cameras from the houses nearby picked up a man in a hoodie running from Mrs. Johnson's house shortly after that 911 call. We figure that Hale must have heard the ambulance sirens and panicked, because he ran. Either way, beating was his MO. We held back some of the details of Lombardi's and Fadil's crime scenes. He beat them before shooting them. We asked the families not to share that detail, and so far, they've complied." Another hesitation. "We think he was trying to get them to share Charlotte's address. That Hale never got to Charlotte's apartment says that they kept her secret. Protected her."

"And died doing so." Tino closed his eyes. "That's going to

—" He nearly said *kill her*, but bit the words off. He couldn't set those words into the universe. "She'll feel even guiltier."

Vito pulled into the prison's parking lot and shut off the engine. "Therapy, bro. She's going to need it."

Nodding, Tino started to get out of the car when his cell buzzed. "It's Nick Lawrence," he said after glancing at the caller ID.

"Put him on speaker," Vito said and Tino did.

"Nick," Tino said. "I'm with Vito and you're on speaker."

"Good. I called you first, Vito, but you weren't in the office. I left a message. I got news from the prison in Memphis where Charlotte Walsh's stalker was killed. They've got a suspect. A few inmates saw the stabbing happen but didn't talk until they were promised concessions. Long story short, they got the killer to admit that he'd been paid by one of the other inmates to kill Charlotte's stalker. Guess who paid a visit to that inmate two weeks ago?"

Tino's heart sank. "Kevin Hale?"

"Bingo," Nick said grimly. "He had the man who hurt Charlotte killed. I don't know how he got any of the information he had, but I thought you should know. Hale must have gone straight to the prison in Memphis after being released."

"He had Charlie's attacker killed before he even saw her in the restaurant," Tino said, feeling sick. "That's even more disturbing. He was focused on her even before he saw her again."

"Looks like it," Nick confirmed.

"Thank you," Vito said. "We're about to talk to Hale's former cellmate. Now we have even more questions to ask."

"Yes," Tino murmured. "Thank you, Nick. I appreciate it."

"Good luck, guys," Nick said.

Yeah. They were going to need it.

* * *

MOUNT AIRY, PHILADELPHIA, PENNSYLVANIA
THURSDAY, MARCH 31, 10:25 A.M.

"I'LL CLEAN THE KITCHEN," Gino said. "You cooked. And it was delicious. I'd feel bad for Tino that he missed it, but I'm thinking you'll cook for him again soon."

Charlotte smiled at him. "I'll cook for you, too. I like cooking for people who like my food. I can help you tidy up."

Gino waved her away. "Go call your aunt. Tell her I said hi. I wasn't an artist like Tino, but I always liked her class."

"I will. Thank you." She took her phone to Tino's bedroom and closed the door behind her. The bed loomed large, and she sank onto the edge. She could smell Tino's aftershave on the sheets. He'd always used the same kind, even back in high school. All the other guys smelled like Brut or Old Spice, but Tino's scent had always been woodsy and light.

She should know. It had been her gift to him the first Christmas they'd exchanged gifts, back in the ninth grade. She'd smelled aftershave products at the mall until her head had ached before choosing the fragrance. That he still wore it gave her a warm feeling, deep in her chest.

He'd given her a small, silver-plated heart on a chain that same Christmas. It currently resided in her safe deposit box, its value purely sentimental.

I should have come home years ago. To Tino.

And to Dottie. She'd been so happy when Charlotte had come back for good. *I'll take care of her for as long as she has left.* Which was hopefully a long, long time.

Charlotte was about to call the nurse's station in the ICU when her phone vibrated in her hand. A FaceTime from Kayla. "Hey, honey. What's—?"

Her words fell away.

It wasn't Kayla. The face that looked out from her phone was the same face Tino had drawn the night before. Kevin Hale.

It took a second for her brain to register the gravity of the situation.

Kevin Hale had Kayla's phone.

The warm feeling that had filled Charlotte's chest was gone in an instant, replaced with cold dread. "Hello, Kevin," she said quietly, not sure of what to say or how to behave.

He smiled, looking pleased. "I knew you'd remember me. This one here, she's a friend of yours, I take it." He turned the phone to one side, revealing Kayla.

Terror stole Charlotte's breath. *He has Kayla.*

The girl was tied to a chair, a gag in her mouth. Weak light filled the room behind her, but it was enough to showcase the bruise that covered the left side of her face.

He'd hit her. Fury mixed with the terror. He'd hit a thirteen-year-old girl. An innocent.

But he'd already hurt so many innocents. Of course he wasn't above hitting a child.

"Let her go," Charlotte whispered hoarsely.

"I will. I promise." He turned the phone back so that his face was all she could see. "Just come to our house, and I'll take her home. And don't tell your *friend*." He said the word with a sneer. "If I see a single cop—or Tino Ciccotelli—anywhere around you, I'll kill the kid."

Charlotte's mind was racing, but no coherent thoughts emerged. "Why?"

The sneer gave way to a cheerful smile. "Because I've got us a beautiful house to live in." The smile faltered, revealing a steely determination. "You'll be happy here."

It sounded like a threat.

"Why me? After all this time?"

He looked hurt. "Charlie, I've been *waiting* for you all this time. You left town and I lost touch with you for a while, but you came home. To me."

She wanted to violently disagree. Wanted to tell him that he was batshit crazy. But he had Kayla.

She drew in a breath. "Tell me where to go. Where is the house?"

His smile turned cunning. "So that you can tell your *friend*? Not gonna happen, Charlie. Ciccotelli had his chance with you, and he blew it. He made you leave. He doesn't get a second chance."

This was insane. *He* was insane.

"Then where should I go?" she asked, her voice shaky.

His expression softened. "Don't be afraid, Charlie. I'll make sure you're so happy. I promise. We'll finally be together, and you'll have everything you ever wanted."

She made herself smile. "I know. You've had a long time to plan."

Something dark flickered in his eyes. "I have. I sacrificed decades for you."

She considered asking what that meant, but he glanced at Kayla and his lips thinned. "I'm sorry," she said meekly. "Where do you want me to go?"

"Take a cab to the parking lot at the Verizon store in Roxborough. Get out and start walking across the parking lot toward the Target. If I see anyone following you, the girl will die. Got it?"

Charlotte nodded. "I understand."

He smiled. "You were always smart."

She drew another breath. "How do I know you'll let Kayla go?"

He frowned. "You don't. But I promised I would, and I keep my promises. You should remember that, Charlie."

She hadn't remembered him until the night before. She'd forgotten him minutes after their last tutoring session. But saying either of those things would make him angry, and Kayla would be the one to suffer.

The girl and her family had already suffered enough.

"Okay. When should I be there?"

His smile was delighted once again. "Leave now. Pay for the cab in cash." The smile slipped. "Leave your car at your *friend's* house."

"How did you know—" She cut herself off because he gave her a stern look.

"I know where you are, Charlie. Back with Tino Ciccotelli. He's no good for you. I tried to tell you that back then, but you didn't listen."

Had he?

She didn't remember.

"I was young then. I didn't listen to anyone."

The stern expression remained. "Well, from now on, you're going to listen to me."

"I will."

"Oh, and Charlie? Leave your phone behind. I'm going to search you when I pick you up. If I find a phone or any other tracking devices on you, the girl dies. Got it?"

She managed to nod. "Yes."

"Yes, *sir*," he corrected. "Say 'yes, sir.'"

She swallowed, her heart beating wildly in her chest. "Yes, sir."

"Good girl. You'll learn. Now hurry. I want you to see our house."

"I . . . I need to pack a bag."

"No, you don't. I have everything you need right here. I will take care of you from now on."

She felt dizzy and realized she'd stopped breathing. She

sucked in a breath and forced another smile. "Okay. I'll see you soon."

"I know exactly how long it will take you to get here. I've already called you a cab. They'll be pulling up outside of Ciccotelli's house in two minutes. I'll give you an extra five minutes of travel time in case you get stopped by a light. And, like I said, if I get even a whiff of a cop, Kayla will suffer."

Charlotte jerked a nod. "Okay. I understand."

He ended the call and she sat for a moment, staring at the phone in her hand.

She was not walking into this like a lamb to slaughter. He didn't intend to let Kayla live. Why would he? *So sacrificing myself makes no sense.*

But she had to play along.

Hands shaking, she called Tino's phone, but it went to voicemail.

Because he's at the prison. They would have made him leave his phone behind. Calling Vito would be just as useless then.

She didn't want to call 911. First, it would take too long to explain this to a stranger, and she'd be late to her rendezvous. He would probably hurt Kayla. Second, Philly PD would send cruisers with sirens blazing, and Kayla definitely wouldn't stand a chance.

Closing her eyes, she called Tino's phone again. She needed him to understand. Especially if she never saw him again. Grabbing his pillow, she held it to her nose and inhaled his scent one more time as his voicemail message played. When she heard the beep, she set the pillow aside.

She'd come so close to getting what she'd wanted since the day she'd walked away from Tino Ciccotelli twenty-four years ago. She wasn't going to give that up without a fight.

"Tino, it's me. Charlie. If I don't see you again, just know that I've always loved you. I never stopped, not in all these years. I'm sorry I'm doing this, but I don't know what else to do. He's got Kayla, and she's just a girl. But you'll figure this out. I trust you. And if you don't, don't you dare blame yourself."

She ended the call, then checked her contacts for the one person who'd be able to get word to Tino and Vito at the prison.

* * *

PHILADELPHIA, PENNSYLVANIA
THURSDAY, MARCH 31, 10:35 A.M.

TINO SAT at the interview table next to Vito, studying Gus Greene. The man was shackled, hands and feet, but he didn't look terribly dangerous. He was, however, serving life for murdering three people—strangling them with his bare hands —so appearances were apparently deceiving.

He'd served fifteen years of a life sentence and had spent three of those years with Kevin Hale as his cellmate. Those years had been Hale's final three of his fourteen-year sentence.

"Mr. Greene," Vito said with a nod. "I'm Lieutenant Ciccotelli with the Homicide Department."

His brother had instructed Tino to remain silent unless he signaled that it was okay to speak. Tino chafed at that, but figured he was lucky to be included in the interview, so he obeyed.

For now.

Greene grinned. "'Mister.' Look at me, getting called 'Mister.' Gotta say, that's been a while."

"This is my colleague," Vito said. "He's a sketch artist. He worked with witnesses to recent violent attacks in the city." He slid a photo across the table. "Witnesses described this man. Kevin Hale."

"Sonofabitch. Kevin, not you, Lieutenant."

"You didn't like him, then?" Vito asked.

Greene gave an exaggerated shudder. "Hell no. He was fuckin' nuts. But, if he was on your side, you were safe in here."

Vito lifted his brows. "He provided protection?"

"Yep. He wasn't cheap, but he was damn good at it."

"How much?" Vito asked.

"Depended. If you were a short-timer, it was favors. Usually redeemable when the guy got out. If you had family who visited, it was favors from them—the family would get Kevin information. If you were a lifer like me, it was fifty percent of whatever you made working whatever job you were assigned."

"Inmate pay ranges from about twenty-five cents to fifty cents an hour," Vito murmured to Tino.

"So Hale was making a pittance off his protection," Tino murmured back.

"Pittance to him," Greene said. "It was a hell of a lot to me. A day's wage won't even buy a bar of soap from the goddamn commissary. Still, I wish the SOB was still here." He held out his arm, showing an angry-looking wound from a recent cut. "Some asshole got me in the exercise yard."

"Sorry to hear that," Vito said. "Tell me more about Kevin Hale."

Greene narrowed his eyes. "And you'll move me to Harrisburg?"

"DA says yes, if what you tell us is verifiable."

Greene scoffed. "So you're not promising anything."

"I'm not allowed to," Vito said. "You know that. But if you help us, I'll do my best to help you get closer to your daughter. That I do promise."

Greene pursed his lips, thinking. Then he nodded. "Like I said, Kevin was a crazy SOB. I mean, really nuts. Like schizo. Should have been medicated. But he could focus, so maybe not schizo. Hell, I'm not a shrink." He watched Tino for a long moment. "I'm still not sure why you're here. You're a sketch artist."

"In case you can describe someone we might be interested in," Tino said, which wasn't a total lie. Not the truth either, but it seemed to satisfy Greene.

"Okay, whatever. Kevin was focused, like I said. You might even say he was obsessed."

"With?" Vito asked.

"A woman. Oh my God." Greene rolled his eyes. "Always the same woman. I feel sorry for the chick if he ever finds her."

"Her name?" Vito asked.

"He called her Charlie. Short for Charlotte, he said."

A chill ran over Tino's skin. He'd expected this, but it still freaked him out to hear. His expression must have shown as much because Greene cocked his head.

"You know her, I take it," Greene said easily.

"He seems to be hunting her," Vito said. "He's killed several people already trying to find her. Put another two in the hospital. One was a seventy-five-year-old woman. Beat her near to death."

Greene scowled. "Now that ain't right. The ones I killed were young and dishonest. Beating an old woman is just wrong."

Tino had to squash the most ridiculous urge to laugh but was able to keep his expression neutral. He hoped.

"I agree—with the last part, at least," Vito said. "What did he say about Charlie?"

"That they were an item in high school. Guy's got to be pushing forty and he's still talking about high school." Another eye roll. "Said she left her boyfriend for him. For Kevin," he clarified. "He said they were going to get married. He was going to buy her this house." A put-upon sigh. "Oh my God. Always about the woman and the house."

"What house?" Vito asked.

"He said he bought her a house. He was so happy with himself."

"While he was still here?" Vito pressed. "He bought a house from prison?"

"Yep."

"Was this one of the 'favors' he negotiated with other inmates' families?" Vito asked, making air quotes.

Greene looked reluctantly impressed. "I thought you'd let that detail fly over your head."

Vito just smiled at him. "How did he buy himself a house?"

Greene hesitated. "If he comes back here, I won't live a single week."

"Harrisburg," Vito said quietly, and Greene nodded.

"Okay. Well, like I said, he dealt in information and favors. One of the inmates was a tiny little guy. So young and way skinnier than me. His mama was worried that he'd die in here, so she agreed—through her son—to whatever Kevin demanded."

"Name of this inmate?" Vito asked.

"He won't know it came from me?"

"Nope."

"Okay. Jason Ruskin. He's really just a kid. Was barely eighteen when he got here. But he comes from money. Was sentenced to three to five. His first day, I thought he'd pass out from the fear. Anyway, Kevin heard that Jason's mama started bawling on her first visit, and that was all he needed to know that he had a sucker."

"So Jason's mother facilitated the home purchase?" Vito asked, sounding skeptical.

Greene shrugged. "I thought the same thing, like what kind of dope was Kevin smokin'? But then Kevin shows me photos of the place. Nice little house with a picket fence. Blue. Gingerbread trim. Bay windows. Tin roof. Cherry tree out front."

Another shiver ran down Tino's spine. That was the same

kind of house he'd told Charlotte that he wanted for them twenty-four years ago. How had Hale known?

"How did Kevin pay for it?" Vito asked.

"I don't know. Robbing a liquor store was what landed him in here, but that didn't seem like it would be enough to buy a house."

Vito nodded slowly, his expression thoughtful. "Did he say where this house was?"

"No, but if your sketch artist wants, I can describe it and he can draw it."

"Yes," Tino said. Because that might be where Hale was hiding.

"In a moment," Vito said, giving Tino a back-off look.

Tino wanted to argue, but he bit his tongue.

"Talk to me about the information Hale got through the favors," Vito said.

"News. Contacts. Places to work when he got out. He wanted to work for a construction company. Wanted to learn to build and fix stuff, so that he could work on his house, but nobody would hire him. Not right outta here. But one of the guys—name's Oscar—got work in a restaurant in the city. Old City, I think. Sushi." He made a face. "I hate sushi. Kevin went to work there after he got out, according to Oscar. Oscar's a nice guy."

Not anymore, Tino thought sadly. Because Oscar Dupree was dead.

"Was any of the news regarding Charlie?" Vito asked.

"Oh yeah. More than half, I'd wager." He shook his head. "But that didn't come from Oscar. One of the other guys' wives would run internet searches on this woman. Charlotte Walsh. Kevin was really furious when she got hurt. Some guy in Memphis broke into her house and stabbed her. Been about a year now. Kevin kept muttering about how the guy was dead as soon as he got out of here."

And now Charlotte's attacker was dead as well. Hale had solicited the man's murder in the Memphis prison just days after his release from the prison in Philly.

"Did Hale keep photos of her?" Vito asked.

"Oh yeah." Greene grimaced. "Kept them hidden so that the guards didn't find them. Jacked off to them sometimes. Groaned so loud, he woke me up too many times. It was not easy being that guy's cellmate, I hafta say."

Tino felt fury slowly burning him from the inside out, but he ignored it. *Stay focused. He'll pay for what he did to Charlotte and Mrs. J and all the others.*

"Pleasant," Vito said with a grimace of his own.

"Right?" Greene agreed. "One was her wedding picture. It was old, a clipping from a newspaper. He'd pasted a photo of his own face over the husband's. Kevin just ain't right."

"I'd say not," Vito murmured. "Did the administration here know about Kevin's protection hustle?"

"Sure. But Kevin never actually hurt anyone. Not bad enough to be reported, anyway. He kind of kept the peace, so the guards let him do it. Just the threat of him was enough to make most of the punks in here back down."

Vito nodded as if that was what he'd figured. "Okay. Can you describe the house?"

Tino opened the sketch pad he'd been allowed to bring in with him. "Ready when you are."

"Like I said, it was blue." Greene began to describe the details, all eerily familiar.

Tino thought he could draw the house without Greene's description, but he waited for the man to recall each detail, sketching as they went along.

Finally, Greene nodded. "That looks exactly like the photo he showed me. You're pretty good."

"You have a good memory," Tino said.

"I'll talk to the DA as soon as I leave," Vito said. "I'll make sure he knows how helpful you've been. Thank you."

Greene nodded, wincing as he stood, his shackles clanking. "I'll hold you to that, Lieutenant."

Tino and Vito sat for a moment while Greene was escorted from the room.

"Hopefully we'll find his house based on your sketch," Vito murmured.

"It was going to be our house," Tino whispered.

Vito frowned at him. "What?"

"When Charlotte and I talked about the future—" He stopped himself, realizing now that *he* had talked about the future. Charlotte had simply nodded. *A dinghy in my wake*, he thought sadly. "When I talked about our future, this was the house I described."

Vito's expression grew intense. "Does it exist?"

"I don't know. It must, because Hale bought it. But it was just a dream to me."

"Let's go. When we find it, hopefully we'll find Hale, too."

They were escorted back to the lobby, but halfway there, the warden came hurrying to them.

"Lieutenant!" he called. "You have a message from a Lieutenant Lawrence."

Tino felt dread descend upon him. "What did he say?"

"Charlotte Walsh was contacted by Hale. He's abducted a girl she knows—the daughter of the victim he shot, but who survived. Said if Miss Walsh came to him, he'd let the girl go."

"Kayla," Tino whispered, the picture coming together with terrifying force. "She's trading herself for Kayla."

"Not exactly," the warden said. "Walk with me and I'll bring you up to speed."

CHAPTER 8

CHARLOTTE PAID the cab driver in cash, just as she'd been instructed. She'd managed to slip out of Tino's house without alerting his brother. At least not until she was already pulling away in the back of the cab.

She'd seen Gino run outside, phone in his hand as he stood on the stoop, yelling at her to wait. She'd told the driver to keep going.

Gino had undoubtedly called his brothers, which was as she'd hoped. It couldn't hurt to have a backup in case Nick Lawrence didn't get through to Tino and Vito.

That Kevin Hale intended to kill Kayla Lewis was a given, but she'd try to give the cops a little time to save the girl. *And me, too.*

Please save me, too.

She started walking toward the Target, nervously watching for Kevin Hale. There were cops here somewhere, too. At least Lieutenant Lawrence had promised there would be.

She'd crossed three-quarters of the parking lot when a black minivan pulled into the space she'd just walked through. The driver's window rolled down, revealing a smiling Kevin Hale.

Charlotte's stomach revolted, making her wish she hadn't eaten breakfast. But she put on her best face and smiled back at him. "Hi. Long time no see."

He tilted his head toward the passenger side. "Get in," he said, his voice lower in pitch than she remembered, but he was still soft-spoken. The quiet manner was odd, coming out of a man who'd killed and hurt so many people.

Fighting the urge to look around for Lieutenant Lawrence's people, she did as he said. She did glance in the back, hoping to find Kayla there, but the back was empty.

"Kayla?" she asked.

His gaze slid down from her face to her chest. "Why are you so afraid?"

She realized she'd pressed her palm to her beating heart, then decided not to lie. "You have a girl I care about tied up. I know she's scared."

"She'll be fine." He skewered her with a look. "As long as you didn't call the cops. Did you?"

"No," she lied. "You told me not to, so I didn't."

"Good." He put the minivan in gear and drove out of the parking lot, making his way back to the busy street. He gave her another up-and-down perusal. "You look good, Charlie."

"I'm old," she murmured. "Forty-two." She felt ninety.

"I'm only a year younger." His hands gripped the steering wheel so hard that his knuckles turned white. "Why didn't you write me from college? You said you would."

She had? She didn't remember that. But it seemed like Kevin Hale remembered everything. "I'm sorry. My parents were getting divorced. Everything kind of . . ." She shrugged. "It was hard. I kind of closed in on myself."

Which wasn't exactly true. She'd suspected the divorce was coming and had felt that her parents would be happier not being married to each other. She'd felt the loss, sure, but there had been far more relief.

"I suppose," he said.

"How are your parents?" she asked, trying to get a read on the man who'd killed and maimed to find her.

He's insane, was her first conclusion. Which was true, but that didn't help her understand what he'd do next.

"Dead," he said shortly.

She wondered if he'd killed them. "How?"

His jaw tightened and he stared at the road, continuing to glance up to the rearview mirror, presumably to watch for anyone following them.

Charlotte hoped that Lawrence's people were good at evading detection.

"Dad drank himself to death while I did my first nine," he said. "Mom took pills while I was inside the second time. She left the house to me."

Play the game. Keep it up long enough for Philly PD to find me. "Our house?"

He shook his head. "No, the house I grew up in. I sold it and used the money to buy our house. I didn't want the old house anymore. Bad memories. Dad was a bastard who liked to hit. That's why I always wore long sleeves to school, even when it was hot outside. I had bruises."

"I'm sorry," she said quietly. And she was. "I wish I'd known. I would have tried to help you."

"Didn't want anyone to know. Hated them both. Didn't want you to hate me because of my folks."

Play the game. "I wouldn't have," she said softly.

"I know, but I was . . . embarrassed, I guess."

She wondered how he'd inherited property while incarcerated—and how he'd managed to keep his inheritance. But she wasn't going to ask because he looked softer, like maybe she could build a bridge between them.

She'd use that bridge to run for her life as soon as she could.

"My father hit my mom once," she said. "She was going to leave him then, but stayed in the marriage for me. They still fought like cats and dogs, and I kept waiting for the day when he'd hit her again. He might have, but she insisted that he didn't."

He sucked in a soft gasp. "I didn't know."

"I didn't want anyone to know. It was easier to wear the mask of the popular girl who had everything."

He hmmed at that as he turned into an alley between a liquor store and a pawnshop, stopping the minivan behind a beat-up old pickup truck. "Get out."

"Why?"

His head whipped around so fast that she shrank back against the passenger door. His expression was one of pure fury. That he'd so quickly pivoted from concern to rage was terrifying. "I said you listen to *me* now. Have you forgotten?"

"No," she whispered. "I'm sorry."

"Sorry what?"

She stared at him for a beat then remembered. "Sorry, sir."

"Good." He got out and rounded the van to her side, yanking the door open. He pulled her out and began frisking her.

Don't flinch. Don't cringe.

"No phone. Good girl," he said, then gathered her into his arms and once again she told herself not to cringe.

Gingerly, she laid her head on his shoulder. His hold tightened for several more beats of her racing heart before he released her. "Let's go."

She wanted to ask where but didn't want to anger him. Then her heart sank as he led her to the pickup truck that was parked in front of them. "Get in," he said, picking her up and tossing her in the passenger seat.

She hit her hip hard and couldn't stop her cry of pain.

He glared at her when he'd climbed into the driver's seat. "That did not hurt."

"My hip," she explained, pressing her fist into the joint. "Messed up from a car accident."

He looked instantly contrite. "I didn't know."

"I use a cane, but I left it behind. I was rattled after you called." That was the truth. All she'd been able to think was that Kayla had already suffered enough because of Kevin's obsession, and Charlotte would be damned if the girl suffered any more.

Leaving the black minivan behind, Kevin started up the truck and drove them out of the alley on the opposite side from where they'd entered. "Oh, right. I saw you with it. Well, you can relax. I'll buy you another cane. But once you've had time to rest, you'll feel better. You won't even need it." He smiled, sending a shiver down her spine. "It's not like you'll be leaving our house for anything. I'll take care of everything."

"Where is our house?" she asked, hearing the quaver in her voice and hoping that didn't anger him.

He didn't seem to notice. "You'll see," he said cheerfully.

She glanced in the side mirror as he headed toward the interstate, taking her away from safety. Taking her away from Tino.

Hurry, Tino. Please find me.

* * *

PHILADELPHIA, PENNSYLVANIA
THURSDAY, MARCH 31, 11:15 A.M.

"SHE CALLED ME," Nick said over Vito's speaker phone.

Tino and Vito had retrieved their cell phones along with Vito's service revolver and they were racing back to the city.

The warden had relayed the basics. Charlotte had gotten an ultimatum from Kevin Hale—come to him willingly or he'd kill Kayla Lewis. She'd reached out to Nick Lawrence after calling Tino and getting his voicemail. She'd known that Tino and Vito were interviewing Hale's cellmate and wouldn't be checking their phones for a while.

Tino had one new voicemail from Charlotte and one from Gino, but he hadn't listened to either yet. He didn't think he had the strength to hear Charlotte's voice right now, and Gino would be telling him what he already knew.

"She said that she didn't want to call 911 because she didn't have time to explain the situation," Nick went on, "but she didn't want to be stupid."

"So she just went with him?" Vito demanded. "How is that not stupid?"

"He has the girl," Nick said quietly.

"She already feels guilty that Kayla's father was shot because of Hale's obsession with her," Tino said, understanding Charlotte's intent even though he vehemently disagreed with her choice. "She won't let Hale hurt Kayla if she can stop it."

"Exactly," Nick said. "I tried to get her to wait, to let me find a female detective who could pretend to be her, or at least put a tracker in her pocket, but she refused. She said that Hale had put a timer on her arrival at their meeting place. If she deviated from his instructions, he'd kill Kayla. Like Tino said, she's not going to give him any reason to hurt the girl on her account."

"How did Hale get to Kayla?" Vito demanded. "I put two uniforms in front of the Lewis house."

Nick sighed. "They're both dead, Vito. Shot in the head. Their bodies were discovered about forty minutes ago, when they didn't check in."

Vito sucked in a harsh breath. "Fucking hell. What are you doing about Charlotte? Did she just meet him with no backup plan?"

"Of course not," Nick snapped, sounding irritated. "I put three unmarked cars in the parking lot where she was to meet Hale. One of my detectives saw her get out of a cab at the Verizon store in Roxborough and walk across the parking lot. A black Chrysler Pacifica picked her up and headed back to Ridge."

He stopped and Tino's gut turned over. "And then?" he rasped.

"And then the minivan pulled into an alley and never came out. My detectives found the minivan parked in the alley with no sign of either Charlotte or Hale. They must have gotten into another vehicle."

"You lost them," Tino said, the words strangled.

"Not entirely. I checked the street cams myself, Tino, and I've narrowed down the possibilities of the vehicle he changed to. It's either a black Ford Taurus, a white Toyota Tundra pickup, or a Chevy Leaf. I've got BOLOs out on all three vehicles."

"Okay," Vito said. "Keep me up to date."

"Of course," Nick said. "What did you learn from the cellmate?"

Vito made a sound of irritation. "That Hale has many contacts in the outside world. One of them helped him buy a house."

Tino tuned Vito out as his brother summarized their interview with Gus Greene, focusing instead on the sketch he'd made of Hale's house. Using the app on his phone, he rendered it from the sketch to a photo and did a reverse image search.

"Vito," he snapped when he got an immediate match. "I found it. His house."

Vito looked over at him, eyes wide. "How? My people just started looking."

Your people aren't as good as I am, he wanted to snarl, but he bit it back. "It's what I do. It's in Chestnut Hill."

He held up the Zillow listing so that Vito could see. The neighborhood was one of Philly's fanciest. Not what Tino had been expecting when he'd started the search.

Vito whistled. "Damn, that's really close to your sketch."

"Give me the address," Nick said. "I'll get personnel on the way."

Tino gave him the home's location, a fraction of his dread giving way to hope.

Don't hurt her. Please, don't hurt her.

"No one engages until we get there," Vito ordered. "Not unless they have eyes on both Charlotte and Kayla." He abruptly pulled to the shoulder, using the emergency access road to cross to the other side of the interstate and merging into traffic going the opposite direction. "Do me a favor, Nick. Check the owner of this house."

"Already on it," Nick said. A few seconds later he grunted in frustration. "Corporation. Fancy one, too. Contact information lists a law firm in Rittenhouse."

"The name of the firm?" Vito pressed impatiently.

"Ruskin and Jewel. Harold Ruskin and Darren Jewel are the senior partners."

"Jason Ruskin was the kid who needed protection in prison," Tino said. "The kid with the bawling mother. Harold must be her husband."

Vito nodded. "I think the firm helped Hale buy this house. We need to bring Mr. and Mrs. Ruskin in for questioning."

"I'll take care of that," Nick promised. "You focus on that slimy bastard, Hale."

Vito ended the call and immediately dialed again. Tino

recognized the name of the woman who answered as Vito's lead detective in Homicide. His brother proceeded to let her know what was happening and that Nick was sending cops to Hale's neighborhood. Vito wanted his detectives to gather at headquarters.

He also tasked them with finding out where Kevin Hale had gotten the money to buy a freaking house in Chestnut Hill.

Which was a damn good question. The house had to have cost the earth. It was also a dead ringer for the one Tino had dreamed about in his youth. How had Hale known?

Had Charlotte mentioned it? And if she had, what had been the context?

He didn't question her loyalty. She would never have had a fling with Kevin Hale. Not while they were together. And he believed her when she said she hadn't thought of the man since high school.

But somehow Hale had known the exact house to buy, down to the gingerbread trim.

Hand trembling, Tino hit play on the message she'd left and lifted the phone to his ear. His eyes filled with tears at the sound of her voice.

"Tino, it's me. Charlie. If I don't see you again, just know that I've always loved you. I never stopped, not in all these years. I'm sorry I'm doing this, but I don't know what else to do. He's got Kayla, and she's just a girl. But you'll figure this out. I trust you. And if you don't, don't you dare blame yourself."

I never stopped loving you either, he thought. *Never.*

Angrily swiping at his eyes, he turned to Vito. "What are we going to do?" he asked, choking out each word.

Vito glanced over at him with sympathy. "*You* are going home. I'll have one of the unmarked cars drive you. I will deal with this."

No way in hell, Tino thought. But if he said that to Vito, his older brother would keep him under surveillance. He might even put him in protective custody. On the other hand, if he agreed too quickly, Vito would know he was lying.

"I have to be there," he insisted. The words were true, but not in the way that Vito would take them. "You have to let me come with you."

Vito frowned. "I don't have to. In fact, I can't. It's against every regulation in the book. You know I want to let you, but I can't. If I don't do this right, Hale could skate on every murder he's committed. Charlotte wouldn't want that."

Charlotte might not want that, but she wasn't here right now. *Because Hale has her.*

Tino didn't want Hale to skate on five murders, either, but he wasn't going to let that number become six. Or seven, because Hale had Kayla too.

Luckily Tino wasn't a cop. He didn't have to follow the regulations.

"Of course she wouldn't want that. But what can I do then?" Tino asked, letting his rising panic charge the question.

"Stay home where it's safe."

"I can't just stay home! He's got her, Vito."

"I know. And I'll get her back. Do you trust me?"

"Of course I do." He trusted that Vito would do everything humanly possible to get Charlotte and Kayla out of Hale's clutches. But his brother would do it by the book. And that would take time.

Vito blew out a breath, his relief visible. "Thank you. I'm going to the station and I'm going to have someone take you home. I will focus the entire department on getting Charlotte back safely. Do you believe me?"

"I do."

"You'll stay home then?"

Tino sighed, the sound as tortured as he felt. "Yes." He hated lying to his brother, but he wasn't going to sit on his hands while a man who'd killed five people and put two others in the ICU had his hands on Charlotte Walsh.

Vito gave him a sharp look then nodded once. "Okay."

Tino cleared his throat. "What are *you* going to do?"

"We can't risk Charlotte or Kayla. And this is a residential neighborhood. We can't risk any of the neighbors. We'll need to evacuate before we begin negotiations."

"He won't let her go," Tino whispered.

"We don't know that. I've done this kind of negotiation in the past and have been successful." Vito reached over to squeeze Tino's shoulder. "I get it. We'll try to trick him out. Surround the house and go in through the back."

Tino clicked on the Zillow link, grateful that the photographs of the house were still attached to the listing even though the house had sold the year before. "It has three exterior doors. There's one in front, one in back and one on the side."

"Tell me about the house."

"Three bedrooms, two baths. It has a basement, but it doesn't have a door to the outside. It has windows—three in the back of the house, two in the front. The basement is unfinished. Just the laundry room and storage."

"Okay," Vito said. "I know how I'll go in."

So did Tino. Checking to see that Vito's eyes were on the road, Tino sent off a quick text to Cliff Gargano.

I need your help. Life or death. Not a joke.

A moment later the reply appeared on his phone. ***Where and when?***

My house, thirty minutes. Park and wait up the street. Not in front of the house. You need to know it's going to be dangerous.

The reply was nearly instantaneous. ***Thirty minutes. I'll see you there.***

Hold on, Charlie, Tino thought. *We're coming.*

CHAPTER 9

TINO SLID into the front passenger seat of Cliff Gargano's minivan, feeling too guilty for words. "I shouldn't have texted you. This could get us both arrested. Or even killed."

The uniformed officer who Vito had tasked with getting Tino home had been quiet and efficient—and full of rightful distrust. He'd eyed Tino as he'd driven him to Mount Airy, all while Tino had been texting Cliff, telling him what needed to be done. The cop was still waiting outside Tino's house on the curb, in case Tino got the bright idea of driving himself to where Hale held Charlotte and Kayla.

Which was why Tino had instructed Cliff to meet him on the street a block away. Tino had snuck out through his back door and vaulted over the fence to avoid the cop.

Now, looking at the baby's car seat behind him, Tino was having all the second thoughts. He had no right to put Cliff in danger. The man had a wife and a child.

But Cliff was holding up his phone, showing the map to

Kevin Hale's blue Victorian with the white picket fence. "We're not getting killed. And my mother always figured we'd get arrested together."

"Not a joke," Tino murmured as Cliff pulled away from the curb.

His best friend glanced into his rearview mirror before looking at Tino. "You think that cop waiting in front of your house knows you're gone?"

"Gino's home. He's going to tell them I'm upstairs, that I took a pill to sleep. I should have asked him to drive me. I got no business putting you in harm's way."

Cliff snorted. "Like Gino could do anything that could get him arrested. He's too nice."

"He really is. I worry that he won't be able to lie if that cop comes looking for me, but it's a chance I had to take."

Cliff sobered. "Tino, I read about the murders in Rittenhouse. I know about Charlie's aunt. My mom told me. I know what this guy is capable of doing. I also know that you've had my back since we were kids. I'm returning the favor."

"You don't have to."

"I know. I'm going to anyway." Cliff set his phone into the holder attached to his dash. The map said they were six minutes out.

Vito would be organizing his troops to surround Hale's house and . . . negotiate.

Hale wouldn't negotiate. Tino knew that like he knew his own name. He also knew that the longer Hale held Charlotte and Kayla captive, the more likely it was that the bastard would hurt them. Both had been through too much. Poor Kayla had seen the man who'd shot her father. She had to be so terrified right now.

And Charlotte . . . *God, Charlie. Just hold on.*

"So," Cliff said easily. "You and Charlie?"

Tino nodded, his heart racing as he contemplated what he was about to do. "Yeah. We're giving it our best shot."

"Good. It's about time. Tell me about the guy who has her."

So Tino did, not caring when his voice broke or when tears leaked down his cheeks. This was Cliff he was talking to. His friend had seen him cry before. Not many times, but definitely when Charlotte had left twenty-four years ago.

"I remember him," Cliff said. "Vaguely, anyway. Weird kid. Watched Charlie all the time back then."

Tino stared at him. "Why didn't you tell me?"

"Sonya said that Charlie wasn't interested in him, and that the guy had a crush, that was all. Didn't seem worth getting you upset over it. You would have punched the kid's lights out and gotten yourself expelled."

Tino hated to admit that Cliff was right. "Probably," he said grudgingly.

"Definitely. We were all a little hormonally crazed back then. Going all caveman over our girls. I would have punched him if he'd looked at Sonya that way. Sonya knows where I am, by the way. I needed to give her the chance to speak, to tell me not to help you. But she told me to go, and that I'd better not get hurt." He gave Tino a wry smile. "I'm to stay with the minivan and be your getaway driver. I'm not to go into the house."

Other people might have been surprised at Sonya's approval, but Tino had known the woman for more than a quarter of a century, so he wasn't surprised at all. "That's fine. I'll go in through the back window into the basement. From the photos on Zillow, it's just big enough for me to get through."

"I brought my tools in case you need them. They're in the back. What are you going to do once you're inside?"

"Disable him."

Cliff lifted his brows. "And how will you do that?"

"I have my gun. I won't use it unless I absolutely have to," he added when Cliff winced.

"You don't have a license to carry that thing, dude."

"I do. I have a concealed carry permit. Because of my job."

Cliff's eyes widened. "You've had threats?"

"Yeah, from family members of the assholes who've been arrested based on my sketches." And there had been many of them. Vito had been right. Tino's work told the cops who to look for. *I've done something good with my life.*

And if Kevin Hale's was the last face he ever sketched, Tino would be okay with that, as long as he got Charlotte out safely first. It was possible that Hale would kill him. The man had known where Charlotte was, had sent a taxi to Tino's house to fetch her. Hale had to be angry that he and Charlotte were back together.

But again, as long as Charlotte was safe, Tino was okay with whatever happened to him.

* * *

CHESTNUT HILL, PHILADELPHIA, PENNSYLVANIA
THURSDAY, MARCH 31, 12:30 P.M.

CHARLOTTE'S GAZE had swept through the neighborhood as they'd driven toward the house, trying to look simply curious and not desperate to find an escape route. But she saw no one out in their yards. And she didn't see any sign of Philly PD.

Kevin had driven around town for an hour, ditching the truck for an SUV before finally heading to the house. He'd well and truly lost Lieutenant Lawrence's cops.

I'm on my own.

"What do you think?" he asked as he pulled into a driveway. "Welcome home."

Charlotte stared up at the house in shock.

It's our house.

The house Tino had dreamed about all those years ago. It was blue with gingerbread trim and a wraparound front porch. It had a tin roof and the cherry tree in the front yard was in full, gorgeous bloom.

It was . . . surreal.

"It's . . ." She turned her stare onto Kevin as he pulled straight into an attached garage, lowering the door behind them with a touch to the opener attached to the visor of the Ford Explorer. "How did you choose this house?" she finally asked.

He frowned as he turned off the engine. "You told me that this was your dream. That one day you'd live in a blue Victorian with gingerbread trim, a tin roof, and a wraparound porch. You'd have a porch swing and we'd sit in it for hours, admiring the blossoms on our very own cherry tree."

Charlotte had absolutely no recollection of that conversation, but she needed to play along. "And you remembered. After all this time."

"I remember every word you've ever said."

Wow. Okay. She made herself smile even as she racked her brain for any memory of that conversation, but there was none. "You're so sweet."

He beamed. "Wait until you see the inside. I had some renovations done. Everything was already pretty new. This isn't a hundred-year-old house. It was built twenty years ago in the Victorian style. I wanted to find a genuine Victorian, but I think this is better. Fewer things we'll have to fix. And we're only the second owners. But the kitchen wasn't good enough for you, not with you being a chef."

"Not anymore," she said, more out of habit. Then cursed herself when he slowly turned to look at her.

"What does that mean?" he asked, his eyes suddenly narrowed and angry.

She decided to be honest. "Just that after my car accident all those years ago, my hip has been less than fully functional. I can't stay on my feet for the hours required to be a chef in a restaurant kitchen. But I love to cook in my own kitchen."

I loved cooking for Tino and his brother. And for Kayla.

He relaxed. "Good. I can't wait for you to cook for me. That will be your primary responsibility."

"Okay," she managed. "Good to know. What are my other responsibilities?"

Please don't say sex. Please.

"Pleasing me," he said seriously. "In all things," he added with an underlying note of menace that made Charlotte want to shudder.

She had to hold herself steady when he cupped her face in one big hand. It felt horrible. Wrong. Her stomach roiled.

But she didn't flinch. Didn't gag. Instead, she leaned into his palm.

Play the game, Charlotte. Save Kayla.

She held the pose until he pulled his hand away. "Take off the wig. We're home now." She obeyed, removing the black wig he'd forced her to put on when they'd changed from the truck to the SUV. "Let's go inside. I want to see your face when you see what I've done for you."

Kevin gripped her arm just a little too hard as he pulled her out of the vehicle, tugging her toward the door into the house.

"That hurts, Kevin."

He tightened his grip substantially, making her try to pull away on reflex. "Can't have you running away."

She had to breathe through the sharp pain. "I promised I wouldn't."

"You also promised you'd write to me from college," he said bitterly. "I waited every day for a letter and none came."

"I told you why," she said patiently. "I was a mess when my parents split up."

"Did you write to *him*?"

Tino. Who probably knew what she'd done by now. "No."

I wish I had. But I didn't.

He hauled her to the door, making her walk far faster than she was able.

"Kevin, I can't walk that fast."

"Sure, you can. And you will." He took the stairs quickly, dragging her with him.

She stumbled and fell, unable to hold back a whimper of pain.

He yanked her back to her feet, setting her shoulder on fire. She pulled back, trying to free her arm.

"You are *hurting* me."

"Shut up," he hissed. "Get in the house." He unlocked the door and, releasing her, shoved her through.

She stumbled again and fell to the floor. It was hardwood and buffed to a slippery shine. She drew a breath, taking a moment to orient herself.

It was a large foyer, the walls painted a dove gray. Somehow that made her feel better, because that was not what Tino had dreamed about. He'd wanted their walls to be robin's-egg blue because it was such a cheerful color.

And it would match Charlotte's eyes.

She was contemplating how to stand up when Hale gripped her sides and lifted her like she weighed nothing. She'd have to use her brain to get out of this, because she was no match for the muscle he'd put on in the twenty-four years since high school.

She placed a hand on the wall to steady herself, only to have it knocked away.

"Have some respect," he snapped. "I painted these walls myself."

Play the game. "I'm sorry, sir. I need my cane."

"Oh." He sounded vaguely apologetic. "Well, come see the rest of the house. I'll get you a new cane later."

She glanced at the stairs and tried not to grimace. The banister was beautifully refinished and the stairs polished to a shine, but she wasn't going to be able to walk up those stairs.

"The kitchen," she said brightly. "I want to see it."

He smiled. "I thought you might. I bought groceries last night, so you can cook for us."

"Of course." She shuffled into the kitchen, trying not to think about how much her hip hurt. And then all thoughts were wiped away when she saw Kayla sitting in a chair at the table, still bound and gagged. Her eyes were wide and terrified, red from crying. She made an agonized noise that had Charlotte rushing to her side.

She started to take Kayla's gag away, but Kevin grabbed her arm again.

"Don't touch her," he snarled.

"All right." He stood slightly behind Charlotte, so she risked mouthing to Kayla. "It will be okay."

Kayla blinked, sending more tears down her cheeks.

"I'm here," she said to Kevin. "Let her go now. You promised."

He chuckled. "I didn't say I'd do it today."

She wasn't surprised. "Has she eaten today?"

"I don't know. I grabbed her from her house."

Charlotte glanced at him sharply. "There was a police guard at her house."

"They're dead," Kevin said flatly.

Charlotte gasped. "You killed them?"

He shrugged. "They were in my way." Then he smiled again,

a malevolent sight. "Enough of that kind of talk. What do you think of the kitchen?"

Charlotte stared at him. "What?"

His smile dimmed, and she took a wary step back. "I had this kitchen remodeled just for you, Charlie. What do you think of it?"

She looked around wildly, willing her brain to cooperate. But he'd killed two cops. And Mr. Lombardi. And Mrs. Fadil. And he'd nearly killed Kayla's father and Dottie.

I have to get us out of here.

She forced yet another smile. "It's a beautiful kitchen." It really was. It looked as if it had leapt from the pages of a magazine. The appliances were all shiny and new. The cabinets gleamed. But she could see that the window was nailed shut. There was a door on the far wall that probably went to the basement. That was a possible exit, but he'd probably locked it, just as he'd locked the door into the garage. *If I can just get his keys . . .* "This is everything I always wanted. Would you like me to make you a nice lunch? Or maybe a late breakfast? What would you like to eat?"

He sat in one of the kitchen chairs, waving his hand like a sultan. "Surprise me."

She opened the fridge, blinking in surprise at how well it was stocked. "Give me a minute to see what I can make. Do you have any food allergies?"

"You don't remember?" Kevin asked.

Charlotte exhaled slowly. "Sir, I don't remember a lot of things since my attack. I had a head injury." It was a lie. She hoped he'd believe it. "So if I don't remember everything, please don't take it personally."

"I bet you remember *his* favorite meal," Kevin muttered.

French toast. "I don't," she lied, opening drawers, familiarizing herself with their contents. Looking for a weapon.

The knife block was conspicuously bare, the empty slots mocking her. There were forks and spoons in the drawers, but not a single knife. Not even a butter knife.

It appeared that Kevin wasn't taking any chances.

"I'll need to chop some vegetables," she said lightly. "But you don't seem to have invested in a single knife."

"I've set them aside," he said. "I'm not sure that I trust you yet. I had to force you to come with me."

She leaned against the counter, giving him her full attention. "You could have simply called me. You didn't have to threaten me by taking Kayla. She's innocent in all of this."

He met her gaze squarely. "I thought you'd reach out to me, especially after your aunt went to the hospital."

Fury geysered up inside her, and she had to breathe to calm it. "I didn't realize that was you. I honestly didn't believe you were capable of hurting so many people."

He didn't blink. "I'd do anything for you. I robbed stores for you. *Twice.* Went to prison for you. *Twice.*"

She swallowed hard. "Why?"

"Because I love you."

She barely managed to control the shudder. "No, I mean why did you rob stores? Is that how you bought this house?"

He laughed. "No, idiot. My father wouldn't give me any money, but I needed to come to you. To bring you home from college. But I ended up in prison."

"And the second time?"

"I wanted to get to you in Memphis. I saw your marriage announcement, and I needed to make you leave him."

"You did that . . . for me?"

"I would do *anything* for you."

"Then let Kayla go. If you do, I'll stay with you. No arguments."

He narrowed his eyes. "You'll stay with me regardless. No arguments."

She willed her hands not to shake. It had been worth a try, she supposed, but she'd known it wouldn't work. "I know. But if you really want to make me happy, please let her go. You can blindfold her so that she can't see where we are, but she's just a child, Kevin. Please, let her go."

"You'll be happy, because you're with me." His gaze darkened. "Now make me happy by shutting up and cooking me a meal. I'm starving."

"Yes . . . sir." Trying not to cry, she turned to the sink, looking out the window over it. Looking for any sign that help was coming.

But no one was coming.

She truly was on her own.

Then I'll find another way. I'll get us both out, me and Kayla. I didn't survive that insane stalker last year only to die at the hands of another insane stalker.

But even as she thought the words, she knew that getting even one of them out would be a near-impossible challenge. Getting them both out?

Kayla first.

Unless . . . What if she could drug Kevin? Make him sleep? Then she and Kayla could escape. What in the kitchen could she use?

"Stop staring out the window," Kevin snapped. "Look at me. Or cook a meal."

She looked over her shoulder, praying she didn't appear as terrified as she really was. Because unless Kevin had stocked his shelves with sleeping pills, the best she could do was to make him a cup of warm milk.

That wasn't going to help her get away.

So now? She'd bide her time. "How about a frittata?" she asked.

Drugged or not, he'd have to sleep sometime. She'd have to wait for nightfall. And then she'd take his keys, unlock the doors, and get the hell out of there.

"With bacon?" Kevin asked.

She feigned indignation. "Of course with bacon. What kind of cook do you think I am?"

"Hopefully a good one," he said sharply.

She was a good cook. An expert with spices and seasonings. She knew what spices complemented others. Which should be used sparingly, lest they overwhelm the meal.

Or the chef.

Her breath caught. Most hot peppers made her eyes water when she chopped them. And pepper spray was made from peppers, right?

She couldn't make pepper spray, but she might be able to fudge a suitable substitute.

I can do this. I can get us out of here.

"You won't be disappointed." Opening the fridge, she began to remove the ingredients she'd need. Milk, eggs, spinach, red pepper.

She nearly shouted in relief when she saw the bag of jalapeños. She and Kayla might just have a chance. "If I can't have a knife, you're going to have to do the chopping. I'm adding spinach and red peppers. Maybe a little jalapeño. Just for flavor."

And for your eyes, asshole.

He was quiet for a moment. "I'll give you a knife and supervise you."

Yes. That was what she'd hoped he'd say.

"I'll be right back," he said, then left the kitchen for wherever he'd hidden the knives. At this point, she didn't care where he hid them. She only needed one.

Quickly, she moved to Kayla's side and whispered in her ear. "I'll try to get his keys and then untie you. Be ready to run, even if I don't follow you. Understand?"

Kayla nodded, her eyes still so scared, it broke Charlotte's heart.

Charlotte hurried back to the counter and was sorting through the dry spices—cayenne, chili pepper, red pepper flakes, habanero powder, ground black pepper—when Kevin returned with one large kitchen knife and one paring knife. Both looked dull, but she'd used worse.

She'd make do with the knives, especially if she could tease them away from him. Once she hit him in the face with her mix of spices, she could plunge the knife into his gut.

Except in his other hand, he held a handgun. The handgun had a silencer. This would be the weapon he'd used to wound Mr. Lewis. To kill Mr. Lombardi and Mrs. Fadil and maybe the two cops as well.

If she angered him enough, he might use that gun on her or Kayla. *Or on both of us.*

Don't think like that. Just bide your time. Make your pepper concoction. Be patient.

He handed her the knife, casually pointing the gun at her chest. "No funny stuff."

"Wouldn't dream of it," she lied, then smiled up at him, hoping she could pull this off. "It's a beautiful kitchen. It's going to be a pleasure cooking in it."

Still holding the gun, his aim still firm, he ran a finger on his free hand down her cheek. "You look good in my kitchen, Charlie."

She felt like her face would crack from the fake smile. "Thank you. One frittata, coming up."

* * *

CHESTNUT HILL, PHILADELPHIA, PENNSYLVANIA
THURSDAY, MARCH 31, 12:40 P.M.

TINO STARED up at the blue Victorian as Cliff slowly drove by. "It's uncanny," Tino whispered.

"Exactly like you used to dream about," Cliff agreed. "That's freaky, man."

"It is." Tino's skin felt unbearably tight. Kevin Hale had been thorough, to say the least.

Cliff reached over and squeezed Tino's arm. "He went to so much trouble for her, T. Maybe he won't hurt her."

But Tino was terrified that that wasn't the case. "He killed people to get to her, Cliff."

Cliff sighed. "I know. What's the plan?"

"Drive around the block and park at the back. I'll climb the fence and break in through a basement window."

"And if he has cameras and sees you coming?"

Tino grimaced. "I don't know. It's a risk I have to take. Maybe he won't be paying attention to the cameras." *Because he's hyper-focused on Charlie.* That didn't make Tino feel any better. "If you need to leave, this is the time."

"I'm here. I have your back." Cliff made a face. "From the safety of the family minivan."

Tino studied the homes as they drove to the street behind Hale's house. "I gave you shit about buying such a fancy mini-van, but right now, I'm glad you did. Your Mercedes fits right in."

"I'll remind you of that later," Cliff said lightly. "Also, we got a great deal and this vehicle holds its resale value."

"Yeah, yeah. I was wrong and you were right."

"Ha!" Cliff crowed. "Say that again." He held out his phone.

Tino laughed, as he suspected Cliff had intended. "Shut up." He sobered as Cliff stopped on the block behind the blue Victo-rian. Luckily the fence between Hale and his backyard neighbor was a standard four-footer. Tino could jump over that in his sleep. "If I'm not out in fifteen minutes, call Vito. He'll yell and scream. Tell him I lied to you about where I was going and why."

Cliff held his gaze. "I will tell him the truth."

Tino's eyes stung. "Thank you."

"Go on. Get Charlie out of there."

Tino glanced in the side mirror as he started to open the van's door, then groaned in frustration. "Fucking hell."

Cliff looked around. "What?"

"Nick's here." The man was jogging up the street towards the minivan. "Lieutenant Nick Lawrence," Tino explained. "He's the one Charlie called because she couldn't reach me or Vito."

Cliff didn't have a chance to say anything because the side door was already opening. Nick jumped into the back seat and closed the door.

"Hey, y'all," he drawled. "Fancy meetin' you here."

Tino scowled, his plan crumbling to dust because Nick had probably already called Vito. "Hey, Nick."

"Tino. Mr. Gargano." Nick nodded to Cliff. "Rookie move, driving by the house. Should have just come straight back here. My guys made you right away. Took less than a minute to run your plates."

Cliff looked nervous. "Sorry?"

Nick chuckled. "I'll bet you are. Tino, boy, what're you thinkin'?"

"That he has Charlotte," Tino bit out. "And Vito will do this by the book."

"That he will," Nick said, but his tone was kind. "Sometimes the book takes a while."

"I . . ." Tino closed his eyes. "He's killed five people, Nick."

"I know."

Tino swallowed hard. "He's not going to negotiate with Vito."

"I know," Nick repeated softly. "What was your plan gonna be?"

Tino twisted in his seat to meet Nick's eyes. "Sneak in through the basement window in the back and get her out. Her and Kayla."

Nick looked thoughtful. "He'll kill you if he sees you in his house."

"I don't care."

"Tino!" Cliff gasped.

Tino glared at him. "What would you do if this was Sonya? The same. I know you'd do the same. But it doesn't matter now. We've been made."

"Hold on," Nick said, then checked his phone. "Excellent," he murmured. He typed something then returned his attention to Tino and Cliff. "You nearly got my detective killed."

Tino blinked. "How?"

"Because she was fixin' to knock on Hale's front door to make sure that it's him. She had a frozen casserole for his dinner. Brought it from her own personal freezer when I called her to help. A welcome to the neighborhood thing. If he saw your friend's license plates, he might be able to run them just like I did. I understand you all went to school together. He'd remember Mr. Gargano, here. He might have taken out my detective. Like you said, he's killed a lot of people, Tino."

Tino hadn't considered that and he should have. "Dammit. I'm sorry. But of course it's him. The house is a match for the one his cellmate described."

"It is," Nick agreed. "But the vehicle he drove into the garage was not one of the ones we were expecting. He must have driven around a while to make sure we weren't following. He switched vehicles again. We had to be sure."

"But it's him?"

"It is."

"He came to the door and your detective didn't shoot him?" Tino couldn't control his tone, but Nick didn't appear upset.

"We didn't have a good line of sight and my detective's assignment was purely reconnaissance. Plus, we might have hit Charlotte if he'd dragged her with him and hidden her behind the door."

Tino jaw was so tight that it hurt. "How long till Vito's ready to act?"

Nick looked troubled. "At least an hour. Maybe two. He's waiting on a SWAT team."

"An hour or two," Tino breathed, his gut a churning mess. "He could hurt her in an hour or two, Nick."

"He could," Nick said steadily.

"And you're not going in?"

Nick shook his head, regret in his eyes. "Vito is in command of this op. My detectives and I are in a support role. Vito says to wait for the SWAT team, so we wait."

Tino glanced over the house they were parked in front of, able to see the peak of the blue Victorian's roof. *I'm not going to wait. I'm going in. Even if I have to walk back here after Nick boots us from the neighborhood.* "Did you evacuate the neighbors?"

"We did. They were unhappy, to say the least."

Tino didn't care how unhappy they were. But at least the neighbors would be safe when he did what he had to do. "Now what?"

"Now I'm going back to my detectives and we will hold the fort until the SWAT team arrives and the snipers get into position. You two are gonna drive away." He opened the van's side door and hopped out. "Always a pleasure, Tino. Good to meet you, Mr. Gargano."

The door closed and Cliff exhaled. "What now?"

"I'm getting out. You're going to drive away, just like he said to."

"Um, no. You can get out. I figured you would. I'm staying right here."

Tino didn't have time to argue. "Okay." He pulled Cliff across the console in a one-armed hug. "Thank you."

"Be careful," Cliff whispered. "I'll be waiting here to get us out of Dodge as fast as I can. Don't get killed. You and Charlie deserve a lifetime together."

We do. Tino was going to make sure of it.

* * *

Chestnut Hill, Philadelphia, Pennsylvania
Thursday, March 31, 12:45 p.m.

Charlotte was startled at the sound of the doorbell. "Are you expecting someone?" she asked.

Kevin shook his head. "Keep chopping. I want to put that knife away."

She kept chopping, but the bell rang again and then a third time. She made a face. "It doesn't sound like they're going away."

Kevin took both knives from her hands before leaning down and brushing a kiss against her lips. "I'll be right back."

"Okay," she said, hoping she'd masked her disappointment at losing the knives. And her revulsion at his kiss.

She waited until he'd left the room before shuddering. Then she got busy, grabbing a bowl to mix the peppery spices with the freshly chopped jalapeño. She'd chopped the entire bag of jalapeños, at least a dozen of them, telling Kevin that she planned to freeze most of it so that he wouldn't have to babysit her knife use in the future.

She hadn't expected him to accept that explanation, but he had.

She dumped the entire contents of each spice bottle into the bowl. The cayenne pepper was fairly intense all on its own. The powdered ghost pepper was the best find. That was super intense. Mixed with all the other spices, she should have a decent weapon in her hands. Especially since most of the spices had come in huge bottles.

Kevin must have shopped at Costco.

Best to minimize the frequency of deliveries if you're keeping a woman and a child hostage, she thought, trying to stay calm.

Opening a drawer, she swept the empty bottles into it so that Kevin wouldn't know what she'd done. Then she held her breath as she mixed the contents, adding most of the chopped jalapeños and their juices. Her eyes were watering like faucets. The mix was potent, but would it be enough?

It has to be enough.

Quickly she put a skillet on the cooktop and started heating some oil. She'd sauté the bell pepper and the remaining jalapeños. If she didn't get a chance to toss the contents of the bowl in his face, she might be able to use the contents of the skillet.

Or the skillet itself. Her right arm was pretty strong—it was her cane arm. She took out a second skillet and placed it on the other side of the sink, just in case she needed a plan B.

She hurried, pulling the bowl full of peppery spices toward her when she heard Kevin's footsteps approaching.

"Who was that?" she asked without turning around.

"A nosy neighbor," Kevin said with the irritation she'd anticipated. "What smells good?"

"I'm sautéing peppers."

His footsteps came closer until she could feel the heat of his body.

Here goes nothing.

Gripping the bowl, she waited until he stood next to the skillet, observing the contents with a frown. He blinked rapidly as his eyes began to water.

"Where are the other peppers? I thought you were going to freeze the rest of them," he said, then turned to face her, and she knew that this was it.

She flung the contents of the bowl full into his face and stepped back, her heart beating so hard that it hurt.

He screamed, his face contorting in pain. "You fucking bitch!" He dropped the knives to the floor but held onto the gun, his now-free hand coming up to rub at his eyes.

Keep rubbing, asshole. That'll only make it worse.

Kevin fired then, the bullet hitting the ceiling, showering plaster on their heads.

Knives. Where are the knives?

Charlotte blinked because her eyes were watering, too. Her lungs were burning and she started to cough. The dust from the spices hung in the air and she was breathing it in.

But so was Kevin. She'd fallen to her knees, feeling around for the large knife he'd dropped when a door slammed open, hitting the opposite wall. It had come from the direction of what she'd assumed was the basement.

"*Holy Mother of God.* Charlie, what did you do?"

"*Tino,*" she gasped softly. Tino was here.

Kevin spun around, pointing his gun in Tino's direction.

"Gun!" Charlotte shouted, her fingers encountering the knife a split second later. She gripped it and, holding on to the table, pushed herself to her feet and grabbed his wrist hard, pushing the gun so that it pointed at the floor. She wouldn't be able to keep him from regaining control of the gun. He was so much stronger than she was. But it might give Tino the time to save Kayla.

"I will kill you," Kevin snarled. "And then I'll kill him."

Charlotte couldn't see anything but murky shadows through the moisture in her eyes. "Not if I kill you first," she promised, stumbling when Kevin yanked his wrist free. He fired the gun and for a moment she waited, holding her breath. But no one cried out, and she could hear Tino quietly reassuring Kayla.

"There. You're free. Run, honey. Go downstairs to the basement. Climb out of the window if you can. There's help outside."

A moment later a hand gripped Charlotte's hair and yanked her forward.

She stumbled sideways into a hard chest, wider than Tino's. She gripped the knife tighter, freezing when she felt the cold barrel of Kevin's gun pressed against her forehead.

"Put the gun down," Tino commanded, but Kevin only laughed.

"No fucking way."

Charlotte put her free hand on Kevin's abdomen. *Right there. The knife goes right there.*

"The house is surrounded by cops, you idiot," Tino snarled. "They'll shoot you on sight."

"Not if I have Charlie as a hostage. And if I can't have her, no one will."

Charlotte thought she'd be sick at the thought. *Stab him. Do it.*

She plunged the knife into Kevin's gut as hard as she could manage.

He roared in pain, tightening his hold on her hair.

This was it. He'd shoot her now.

But then came a clanging sound and Kevin took one faltering step forward before falling to the floor, dragging Charlotte with him. She landed on her hands and knees, moaning as her hip jolted, the pain echoing throughout her body.

A new scream erupted from Kevin and, though her vision

was fuzzy, she could see that he'd fallen face-first, driving the knife deeper into his gut.

She looked up to see Tino standing above them, holding the skillet from the stovetop. He put the skillet back on the stove and bent to lift her gently.

"You okay?" he rasped.

"Can't breathe. Need to get outside."

He slid an arm around her waist, helping her walk from the kitchen, but she shook her head. "Get his keys," she said. "And his gun."

"Got his gun already. Grabbed it when I hit him with the pan. Where are his keys?"

"Check his pocket."

Tino let her go, but was back in ten seconds, although it felt like ten hours. "Found them. Kayla! Are you still here?"

Footsteps thundered up the stairs. "I couldn't reach the basement window." There was a pause. "Is he dead?"

"I don't know," Tino said, "but we're getting out of here."

Charlotte dragged herself to the front door with Tino's help. Everything hurt, but she was free. Tino had come.

A moment later the lock clicked and the door opened.

Cool, sweet air filled Charlotte's lungs, but they still burned.

Everything burned—her eyes, her lungs, the inside of her mouth and down her throat.

"I may have overdone the spices," she muttered.

Tino's laugh sounded choked. "Maybe."

He helped her down the front porch stairs, Kayla taking her other arm.

"You okay, honey?" Charlotte asked Kayla.

"Yeah." But the girl was still crying. "He didn't hurt me, but he killed those cops at our house."

"I'm so sorry, honey," Charlotte said miserably, then coughed.

She could hear shouts and opening doors, but they sounded kind of far away. Across the street?

"Not your fault," Kayla said. "It's *his*. That asshole in there. Is he dead?"

"Don't know," Tino said. "Don't care. All I care about is that you two are safe."

"Where did you come from?" Charlotte asked.

"Basement," Tino said. "The cops were going to have to try to negotiate with the bastard. I couldn't wait for them to try."

"He was going to keep me forever," she said dully, because now that this was over, the adrenaline was crashing. "He wouldn't have let me go. I need to sit down."

Then she did, her legs collapsing beneath her. Tino and Kayla kept her from hitting the ground too hard, slowly lowering her to her knees. They sat beside her, helping her situate herself so that she sat on her butt. The ground was cold and wet, but she was free and she would never complain again.

"Oh my God. *Tino Ciccotelli.*" An angry male voice was snarling at them.

"Vito," Tino said evenly. "So Nick called you?"

"He did. Told me what you were planning. What the fucking hell do you think you were doing?" Vito raged.

Tino's sigh was weary. "What I had to. I'm sorry, but I couldn't wait for you to do it by the book."

Charlotte squinted up at Vito. He was still just a fuzzy figure. "He saved my life. Don't yell at him."

Vito grunted. "I'll yell at him later when you're not around to listen. I've called an ambulance. Are the three of you okay? What happened to you?"

"Homemade pepper spray," Charlotte said. Her chest convulsed in another bout of coughing. "Kevin's in there. I stabbed him."

"And I hit him with a skillet," Tino added. "He might be dead, but I doubt it. Here's his gun."

Blinking hard, Charlotte saw him pass the weapon to Vito.

Vito was frowning. "You have another gun, Tino."

"I do. It's mine. Got a concealed carry permit. I'm legal."

"Did you use it?"

"No." Tino sounded embarrassed. "In all the confusion, I kind of forgot and the skillet was just there."

"At least you didn't shoot him," Vito muttered. "You made pepper spray, Charlotte?"

Charlotte only nodded, figuring that they'd find the evidence of what she'd done. She didn't want to talk about it anymore.

"It's intense in there," Tino said. "You should wear a gas mask or a respirator when you go in to get Hale."

Vito began directing his people to protect themselves before entering the house, then knelt in front of them, scowling at Tino. "Nick said you went through a basement window."

"Nick is a tattling bastard," Tino said. "The windows were nailed shut. I had to break the glass, but the window was just big enough for me to fit through."

"Are you cut?"

"Not much. Worth it, anyway. I got up to the kitchen and freed Kayla. Charlotte had already let loose with her pepper mixture."

"Kevin would have killed me," Charlotte murmured. Of that she had no doubt. There was no way she could have kept up the act indefinitely.

"We'll take care of him," Vito assured her. "Kayla, this is Detective Joanne Perkins. Go with her, and she'll let you call your mom. She's been worried sick."

Kayla's presence disappeared, and Charlotte closed her eyes. It was done. "I did it."

Tino's hand engulfed hers. "You did. I'm so proud of you. You were scared, but you used your head. You're a superstar, baby."

She rested her head on his shoulder. "I need a shower. I have pepper in my hair."

Tino laughed quietly. "I'll take care of you. Don't worry."

She believed him.

EPILOGUE

"He's beautiful," Charlotte murmured, looking down at the bundle she carefully held.

Sophie had held on for another fifteen days before going into labor, long enough that the doctor was satisfied that the baby would be fine. Sophie would be fine as well, she'd assured them, but Vito was ever watchful.

The family had come to meet little Harry in shifts, and it was Tino's turn. He'd insisted Charlotte accompany him, even though she hadn't thought she should be included.

Tino had been adamant, though. Partly because he wanted her to be a part of his family, as she should have been all along. And partly because he still didn't want to let her out of his sight.

He was getting better about the second one. But he didn't think he'd ever forget the sight of that monster putting his gun to Charlotte's head. That the man had died in the hospital of the wound to his gut didn't keep Tino awake at night.

But it did keep Charlotte awake. She'd dealt the death blow

and she went through periods of relief, pride, and guilt in equal measure.

The pride was well earned. She'd been resourceful and brave, using the items in Hale's kitchen cupboards to take a madman down. She'd gotten justice for those Hale had wronged.

Philly PD had mourned the two officers Hale had killed to get to Kayla Lewis. Tino had never met them, but Vito said the fallen officers had been good men and good cops.

The inmate who'd killed Charlotte's stalker had confessed to taking direction from another inmate, one with whom Hale had met at the Memphis prison. Hale had paid a thousand dollars for the stalker's murder. Tino wasn't exactly devastated that the man was dead, because it meant that he could never hurt Charlotte again.

Oscar Dupree, the man who'd helped Hale get a job at the Japanese restaurant, had been murdered for his money, and that had puzzled Vito for a while. But then Vito had discovered that Kevin Hale's inheritance from his mother had been in a trust controlled by the family of the rich, skinny kid that Hale had been protecting in prison. Hale had hired them to manage the trust his mother had left him, selling his parents' house and buying the blue Victorian.

But the money was all gone. What remained after the house purchase had been taken by the state, who charged inmates for their prison stay. Turned out that fourteen years at fifty bucks a day added up.

That was why Kevin had needed the job at the restaurant to begin with. Had he not bought the blue Victorian with cash, he would have had enough to live comfortably for decades.

Kayla Lewis's father had been brought out of his induced coma and was making some progress toward recovery. It would be a long road for that family, though. They didn't blame Charlotte for Hale's obsession with her, but Charlotte blamed herself.

She'd been cooking like a woman possessed, making sure that the three families impacted by Hale's shooting spree on her street would not miss a single meal. The rest of the time, she was caring for her aunt, who'd been discharged from the hospital only a few days before. Mrs. J wouldn't fully recover, but she was in much less pain. Tino and Charlotte had told her a very toned-down version of the story of Kevin Hale, but even that had required doctors to treat Mrs. J for a mild heart attack.

The elderly woman was very excited that Charlotte and Tino were back together, however, and that was what Charlotte had emphasized. She'd moved her aunt into her condo partly because, even with a stair lift, Mrs. J wasn't able to navigate the stairs alone.

But mostly because Mrs. J didn't feel like she could live there again, not after having been attacked there. She liked Charlotte's condo and was already planning on helping Charlotte cook for the neighborhood.

But for now, Mrs. J was taking it easy, mostly watching television and snoozing. Tino had fetched art supplies from her house for her to enjoy when her broken arm was healed.

"Are you and Uncle Tino having kids?"

Tino blinked at the question, asked by Sophie's oldest. Anna was seven years old and as chatty as her mother, but with the bluntness of her father.

"Anna," Sophie scolded from the hospital bed. "That's a private matter, between Charlie and Tino."

Anna looked confused but apologized to Charlotte.

Charlotte glanced up at Tino before smiling at Anna. "It's fine. I understand why you'd be curious. But I think, for now, I'd be happy visiting with you and your brothers. Maybe I can come by and we can make dinner for your mom so she can rest. I'll show you how."

Anna was more than satisfied with that answer. "Beef bour-guignon?" She butchered the pronunciation, making Sophie wince.

Charlotte laughed. "Of course. I'll show you how. I've already made your dinner for tonight, but you can help me make tomorrow night's dinner."

Tino fought his own wince at that. Making dinner for Sophie and Vito's brood would mean going to Vito's house, which meant another verbal assault from his brother. Vito still hadn't forgiven him for breaking into Hale's house.

Tino was okay with that, though. If they'd waited on negotia-tions, Charlotte might have been dead. Which even Vito accepted, but he was still pissed off.

He'd get over it. Eventually.

"Charlie wiggled out of Anna's question about kids pretty well," Vito whispered from beside him, making Tino jump. Vito hadn't been there when they'd arrived, and he hadn't heard him approach.

"No kids," Tino whispered back. "We talked about it already."

Vito's brows went up. "Already?"

Tino kept his voice so quiet that no one could overhear. "She wanted to make sure I understood her limitations. Even if we weren't forty-two, her attacker stabbed her in her abdomen. The damage was so severe that she can't have kids." He'd seen the scars when they'd made love but hadn't realized what they meant. "She said she needed me to be certain I was okay with a future different than the one we'd envisioned as teenagers. Or that *I'd* envisioned, anyway."

Vito nodded, understanding because Tino had shared—

with Charlotte's permission—the reasons she'd had for leaving him back then.

"Did she ever remember how Hale knew about the dream house?" Vito asked, still in a whisper.

"She didn't. Sonya did." Cliff's wife had been able to provide a key piece of information that Charlotte hadn't remembered. "Sonya and Charlie were friends back then. Not best friends like Cliff and me, but they talked. Sonya remembered Charlie telling her about the blue Victorian with the picket fence about a month before graduation. She said, looking back, she could see that Charlie felt trapped, but she didn't realize it at the time."

"You were all only eighteen."

"I know," Tino said, but he could now see how very little he'd listened to Charlotte back then. How he'd just assumed she'd wanted the same things he did. And, even though Charlotte could have and *should* have said something, he mourned his own teenage stupidity.

"Anyway," Tino murmured, "it was over lunch, and Sonya remembers 'the creepy kid' hanging around their table. Hale was always following Charlie and sitting close to wherever she was. Sonya thinks that Kevin overheard them talking about it, about the lives they'd live after graduation."

"So . . . you interested in buying a blue Victorian? I hear it's going for cheap."

Tino threw his brother a dirty look. "Not funny, V."

"That's what you get for risking your life by going into Hale's house, you asshole." Vito had returned to normal volume, which was a mistake.

"Vito!" Sophie scolded from the bed. "Children."

Anna's expression was identical to her mother's as she turned to face Vito. "Yes, Daddy, children." Gently she covered the newborn's ears with her hands. "No swearing in front of the baby."

"I promise," Vito said soberly. "I'm sorry."

"No, you're not," Tino muttered.

"No, I'm really not."

Charlotte rolled her eyes at them both as she gave the baby back to Sophie. "We're going to let you rest. Don't worry, Tino and I will take Anna home. I've got dinner all made, and we'll make sure everyone eats."

Sophie smiled up at Charlotte. "Thank you, Charlie."

Charlotte smiled back. She liked it when they called her Charlie, and Tino made it a point to do so every time he called her name. It was a tie to their past, a small way for them to regain what they'd once had.

But Tino figured what they had now was better.

Vito kissed Charlotte on the cheek. "Thank you for taking care of my bunch. My dad is home with Michael." Vito's son had already fallen in love with Charlotte. "They're both looking forward to your cooking."

"I like your dad," Charlotte said. "I always did. We'll take care of him, too."

That she was taking care of everyone but herself was evident, but she'd told Tino that this was what she needed right now. To be useful. It helped keep the dark thoughts at bay.

So Tino would take care of her while she cared for others.

They set off down the hospital hallway toward the elevator, Anna skipping ahead of them.

"I talked to my investment manager today," Charlotte said conversationally. "Dottie wants to sell her house and pool our money together. I don't want to take her money, but selling her house will let me take care of her. My investment guy says that with that money added to the settlement I got from the newspaper who leaked my address, I don't really have to work for a while."

Tino stared at her. "First, that's amazing. Second, does this mean you won't be reviewing restaurants for the foreseeable future?"

"Yes, that's what it means. But I think I'd decided to stop anyway. My heart hasn't been in it for a while. If I'm too scared to give a negative review, I'm pretty much done. My therapist says I don't have to prove to myself that I can do it. That I proved enough to myself by taking down Kevin Hale. With your help, of course."

Tino agreed with her therapist. He'd been worried about her drawing the attention of the wrong person with a negative review. "But you'll be bored senseless within a week."

"I know. So I looked into volunteer opportunities. Specifically teaching cooking classes at the youth center. I can set my own hours, and once Dottie's more mobile, she can come with me. She misses teenagers, believe it or not."

He smiled. "She'll always be a teacher in her heart."

"Exactly. I'm pretty excited about the idea, too."

She looked it, her eyes alight with an anticipation he hadn't seen since they'd been reunited.

"You'll need a taste tester for your curriculum," Tino said, making her grin.

"You volunteering?"

"Absolutely." He pushed the button for the elevator. "Are you happy, Charlie?"

Her grin became a sweet smile. "I am. Thank you for asking."

"I didn't before, but I'm paying attention now."

"I think we're going to be okay."

He tipped her chin up and kissed her. "I think you're right."

ABOUT THE AUTHOR

Karen Rose is the award-winning, #1 international bestselling author of more than thirty books, including the bestselling Philadelphia, Baltimore and Cincinnati series. She has been translated into twenty-three languages, and her books have placed on the *New York Times*, the *Sunday Times* (UK), and Germany's *der Spiegel* bestseller lists.

She can be found at karenrosebooks.com

www.ingramcontent.com/pod-product-compliance
Lightning Source LLC
Chambersburg PA
CBHW071145131224
18949CB00010B/341